Lock Down Publications and Ca$h
Presents

THE STREETS WILL NEVER CLOSE 4

NEFARIOUS PYT

I0564749

Written By

K'AJJI

First Edition 2024

Printed in the United States of America

This is a work of fiction. Names, characters, places, and incidents either
are products of the author's imagination or are used fictitiously. Any
similarity to actual events or locales or persons, living or dead, is
entirely coincidental.

Lock Down Publications
P.O. Box 944
Stockbridge, GA 30281
www.lockdownpublications.com

Like our page on Facebook: Lock Down Publications
www.facebook.com/lockdownpublications.ldp

Stay Connected with Us!

Text **LOCKDOWN** to 22828 to stay up-to-date with new releases, sneak peaks, contests and more…

Like our page on Facebook:
Lock Down Publications

Join Lock Down Publications/The New Era Reading Group

Visit our website:
www.lockdownpublications.com

Follow us on Instagram:
Lock Down Publications

Email Us: We want to hear from you!

Chapter 1

Moo

Doe and I rode through the streets of Milwaukee after laying low for a few weeks. We hadn't heard anything about the havoc we'd caused, and figured it was safe to come out and get back to business. Ridin' low in Doe's tinted Ford Taurus, we were on our way to see two of the finest hoes off Chambers. However, they love setting niggaz up, killing and moving product. They'd paged bruh and put in the numbers *669*. M-N-Y was their code for money. They had another lick. When Doe called back, Yetta simply asked that we come by the spot. Since she wouldn't tell 'em what was going on over the phone, we were on our way. In my opinion, they'd been acting strange as fuck every since Wintress came home from the hospital. Pulling up on 27th in Center, everything looked normal. We'd jumped out to see niggaz grinding throughout the block as usual.

"Moo, Doe! What up, niggaz?" we heard Smoke yell from down the block as he walked in our direction. Since he's one of ours off the deck, we paused to holla at 'em for a minute. As he walked up, I said: "Shit, chillin', nigga. What's happ'ning?" We shook up.

Smoke said, "You know, gettin' this block money. I don't think Win or Yett 'nem up in that piece. It ain't been no lights on or nothin' goin' on in that mutha-fucka all day."

Doe said, "Yeah, they in there. I just talked to Yetta about twenty minutes ago."

"Oh, a'ight then. Tell they stankin' asses I know they heard me knockin."

"A'ight, will do," I replied, looking over my shoulder as I walked up the stairs leading to the porch. "Where Thirty and Brew at?" I asked.

"Aw, dem fools ran around to Zu-Zu's to grab some Little Debbie's and shit. Niggaz got the munchies." He laughed.

"Y'all good on work?" Doe asked, looking at his pager after feeling it vibrate.

"Yeah, we still holdin'."

"A'ight, hit me when y'all ready. We gotta holla at lil' mama nem on some business real quick. Make sure don't nobody come to the door, a'ight."

"A'ight, I gotchu," Smoke replied.

Doe unlocked the door and we stepped inside. Looking to our left, we saw Wintress sitting in the dark. The only reason we saw her was because she'd taken a drag from her Newport and it illuminated her face.

Doe said, "Girl! Turn some lights in this bitch!"

"What? You hidin' or some shit?" I asked, flicking the light switch on.

Wintress was sitting on the couch with her legs crossed. As she rocked them back and forth, she took another pull from her cancer-stick. She wasn't wearing anything but her panties and bra. The panties and bra, along with her chocolate skin, were covered in blood spatter. Sitting next to her on the cushion of the couch, was a bloody Bulldog foe-foe.

I said, "Wintress, what the fuck happen? Where Yetta?" Doe and I both pulled our thumpers.

She said, "She a'ight. She upstairs. Y'all can put them gunz up. We got this."

"Y'all got what, crazy ass girl?" Doe asked.

"Shhhh! Boy, damn! Yettaaa!" she called out to her girl. She then leaned forward. Putting her square out in the ashtray, she grabbed her gun. She was on the verge of standing when we both pointed our guns at her. We didn't know what the fuck was going on.

She said, "What tha'fuck! Uh-unn! I know y'all didn't! Here, boy!" She handed Doe her gun. "All these years! If y'all still can't trust a bitch, I don't need to be fuckin' with y'all. C'mon! We got something to show y'all upstairs."

We followed as her five-foot-six frame led the way, ass jiggling in stride. When we'd made it upstairs to Yetta's door, she tapped on it lightly.

"Yetta! Bitch, you heard me calling you!" She twisted the knob and pushed the door open.

What we saw had us stunned for a second. She too wore nothing but her panties and bra, which were also covered in blood. Some nigga was stretched out and tied to the bed. His head look to be three times its normal size. Blood was everywhere.

Yetta said, "Damn, took y'all niggaz long enough. Shit!"

Doe said, "What the fuck is this? I thought y'all called us about some money!"

"That is money, nigga. You better recognize. That's Atkinson's finest!" Yetta replied. "And ooh! Y'all won't believe what he had in store for y'all asses. Y'all owe a bitch." She shifted her weight from side to side.

"Nah, two bitches. Geh me my damn gun, Doe!" Wintress hissed, snatching it from his hand.

Smacking her lips, Yetta waved us off. She said, "His lips all swollen. He ain't gon' be able to tell y'all, so allow me. The nigga came at us last night on some fuckin' shit at first. He said he had five-thou apiece for me and Win to bust down and give him a threesome. Say he want some head, some pussy, and some ass. We like, cool."

"Who is that?" I asked, because I still didn't recognize him. "You say he from the hood?"

Yetta said, "Look close."

"Then!" Wintress tried to butt in, but Yetta cut her off.

"Hold on, let me tell 'em. Then, this foul ass nigga get on some real live fuck shit. Talking about let him run up in the spot and act like somebody robbed it type-shit. Tom-bout we can split the money 60/40."

Wintress said, "Yuuuup! Sho-in-the-fuck-did!"

"We fucked and sucked his ass to sleep after we got that money. And, when his punk-ass woke up this mornin'!"—Yetta clapped her hands—"Ta-dahhh!" She smiled.

Doe said, "Aw, fa-real! Is the nigga dead? Y'all ain't kill'em, did y'all?" He took a step towards the bed, but Wintress stopped him.

She said, "Hold up, let me see." Walking over to 'em, she whacked him across his face with the Bulldog so hard that me and bruh both winced.

"Dayuuuum!" we said in unison.

She said, "Goldie! Wake yo' bitch-ass up, nigga! You got company!" He was awake, but dizzy, his eyes bulging out of his head at the sight of us.

Yetta said, "We couldn't get no info out his ass, so I'm glad y'all came. I need a break. I'm hungry. I want a McRib." She pouted.

Doe laughed. "Huh? You hungry? Go getchall crazy asses in the shower while we holla at this nigga! We'll getchall something to eat in a minute." They left the room. Walking over to the bed, I said, "What up, homeboy?"

"Yeah, ain'tchu glad to see us?" Doe greeted him with a sinister grin.

Chapter 2

Gina

I know Cupcake has ill feelings towards me, but I've gotta warn her somehow. I've got a number for her, but I don't wanna call and risk leaving a paper trial that can eventually be traced back to me. I've gone from hood to hood in search of her ass, and I'm exhausted. Though nobody knew it, I'd been looking for my sister ever since the frightening discovery of what was left of Fatima's body. As suspected, she seemed to have disappeared, and I'm glad because if I can't find her, neither could anybody else. I hadn't told a soul about what I'd found. I couldn't. But, in my heart of hearts, she's my number one suspect. Crime Technician found what they believe to be skin tissue under Fatima's fingernails. It was explained to me that the state lab now awaits the results of what they're calling a PCR DNA test. It's all new to me. I'm just praying her chromosomes aren't a match in this so-called DNA database. An unexpected lead fell in my lap when the Tech reports came in. They'd also pulled a set of prints at the scene that couldn't be paired to family nor friend of the home owner. I was thrilled to learn that the prints had come back to one of J.L.'s henchmen, and they weren't Cup's. His name is Russle Shine. He's known to the streets as Hussle. He too is missing. We've got a warrant out for his arrest, which he's more than likely aware of. We'd raided his mother's and his girlfriend's homes in search of him. The brass is all over my Captain's ass, so he's straddling mine.

The department dealing with a string of unsolved murders ain't a good look. They want results. I'm pulling up to CPS now. Though it's been weeks, Child Protective Services still has three-year-old Nomi Waters in their custody. His case worker has finally agreed to allow me to meet with him. I got a whole lot of nothing out of his mother; besides, she'd talked Fatima into coming home to celebrate what would've been her 24th birthday. Sadly, she'd died a few days shy of ever seeing it. The bitch told me that much, then lawyered up on me. It makes me feel like there's more to it. Like she's hiding something. While walking inside the building downtown in the six-hundred block of Wisconsin Avenue, I found the glass doors and tan walls welcoming. I'm thanking God that I don't need Alexus' permission for this interview. Dr. Janis Stall will be sitting in recording the session. I stepped to the receptionist at the front desk. She looked to be in her forties.

"Hi, I'm Detective Burke. I'm here to see Doctor Stall and Nomi Waters. How's he doing?" I asked the white blond woman behind the counter. She'd glanced up at me for a moment, then turned her attention back towards her computer screen.

She said, "The doctor is expecting you. I haven't had the pleasure of meeting Nomi. But, I'm sure he's fine." She hit a few keys on her server, then looked at me and smiled. "Please, have a seat. I'll notify the doctor and let her know that you've arrived." I took a seat. Crossing my legs, I patiently waited as she rang the doc.

Moments later, I was greeted by Dr. Stall. She's surprisingly pretty, and a black woman like myself. She'd sounded as white as Christmas over the phone. In her hand was a *Sam-I-Am* coloring book, and a box of Crayola crayons. She handed me both.

"Follow me," she said, giving me a look of assurance. I did as she'd asked.

"How is he?" I asked. She turned back towards me slightly as I followed.

"He misses his mother, and he wants to go home. She's here on a daily. Hasn't missed a beat. In my objective opinion, I'd say he's normal for any child that's been through this sort of trauma. I think he's doing very well."

I couldn't believe I was about to interview this child about this unspeakable violence.

Chapter 3

Cyn

Well, Money mad at me right now. But I might as well keep tellin' y'all. Miraculously, the nigga—Action—didn't die. One of Bri's slugs went through his jaw and lodged in his wisdom tooth. Let's just say the other one did damage to the brain. But not enough to make him forget what we'd done to 'em. He was released from the hospital after eighteen months and twenty-two days; and he came straight at us! We'd rented *The Rave* to celebrate Mula's 18th birthday. We'd paid Queen Latifah, Shirley Murdock, Bobby Brown, and Eric B. and Rakim to come do a few songs. The twins put everything together for us. It was crackin' so mutha-fuckin' hard! Y'all don't hear me! Listen, Shirley closed the show. She was blowin' *As We Laid*. We sang along and watched the performance from the V.I.P. section as her voice demanded attention.

As we lay, we forgot about tomorrow as we lay / As we lay, didn't think about the price we had to pay—

Shirley bellowed. Every couple and secret lover in the building held that special someone close.

"S-a-a-a-a-a-ng, girl!" Mula yelled, holding up her flute of Chardonnay. She was the drunkest I'd ever seen her. It was her night. Bri was all over Bobby. When we ran into him backstage, she screamed, "Oh-h-h-h-h-h, bay-bee!" She'd ran and jumped in his arms, wrapping her legs around him as if he was her long lost love. He hugged her like he actually knew her ass too! Dressed in all black, his mischievous smile, Gumby and powerful chocolate skin tone, combined with the lyrics, had the ladies going to the extreme!

They were falling out, taking their panties off and throwing 'em on stage and all kinds of crazy shit. Not me though. That shit's unladylike. We were all dressed in the finest linen. I had my hair cut in a Chinese bob. I was in a River Island dress that hugged my curvaceous frame, and yellow-rican skin. You know me. The ass is always standin' up vigorously, healthy and plump. As I walked past, Bri was sitting in Bobby's lap. I said, "Oooh wee! Bri, I see you lovin' you some Bobby." She smiled. Then, knowing we were all together, his foul ass said, "Sup, baby? Damn, you are breathtakingly beautiful. Maybe all three of us can—" He'd reached for my waist, but I smacked his lil' fingers.

Rolling my eyes, I said, "Tuh! Thank you! But no thanks." I kept it movin'. I heard Bri snappin'.

"Sonovah bitch!" The nigga was trying to fix what had just escaped his lips.

"Nig-guh-pleeeeeze! So you think! You think you can—" She threw her drink in his face, and got up and walked off on his ass. Hood was sitting there.

"Mutha-fuckah!" said Hood, sucking her teeth. "Yo' simple ass! I oughta—" She flinched at him, but she didn't swing. She just mugged him, and got up and went after Bri. I then heard Hood yelling at Bri, telling her nothing but the truth.

"Fuck that bitch-ass-nigga! You don't know that nigga! His whorish ass will be in another city or state tomorrow runnin' that same bullshit to somebody else! Getcho shit together! You drunk!"

Sweets and Lue were chillin'. We'd promised auntie that we wouldn't let Lue smoke nor drink anything. Surprisingly, she let her come. And since Lue couldn't do shit, Sweets decided to practise sobriety as well. Thank God for 'em! They were the ones that brought it to our attention that there were a few niggaz in the crowd that hadn't taken their eyes off of nan one of us all night long. And these weren't looks of lust. They felt that the niggaz were up to something. Sweets and Lue said, though one of the niggaz was wearing a snap-back and frames and looked a little diferent, they could've sworn one of the dudes was Action. Mind you, we thought this nigga was dead. We'd find out otherwise firsthand. To be sure our sisters weren't trippin', we had no choice but to try to get close to the niggaz and see for ourselves. We couldn't tell from a distance. However, as soon as we'd got together and came up with that decision, the lights were coming on. The dudes Sweets and Lue were talking about had disappeared in the crowd of those exiting. Hood had dipped off, but now she was back, and clutchin'. When she found out we'd lost 'em, she was pissed!

"Karm and Lue, I thought y'all was gon' keep an eye on 'em! Damn!" she griped, searching the patrons' backs as they left the building. It was dark as hell in there, and the strobe lights didn't help. We couldn't really tell what they'd been wearing. So, the lights being on didn't make a difference.

"Dar he is!" Mula yelled in a drunken slur, she pointed. We'd all looked. "N'all, dat ain't him," she corrected, hugging my neck and shoulder. She was barely able to stand.

She was a hot mess. Her eyes searching the crowd, Sweets said, "They was just right here staring! I don't know what happened that quick. Maybe we saw a ghost."

Hood said, "I just paged Moo and Doe. Them and 3C should be here in a minute. And nah." She shook her head, "Em-mmm, both of y'all ain't seen no damn ghost. I don't believe in 'em. And bitch, why y'all ain't say shit earlier?"

I said, "Hood, we strapped! We don't need them niggaz!" The club was clearing out fast.

Lue said, "Cyn, you right, but we don't know who, or how many niggaz out there."

Bri said, "Yeah, we gotta know who the targets are. You never know what nigguh gunnin' fo' yo' ass. We can't just go out there blind."

Hood said, "Exactly. It's one way in, and one way out this bitch. If they want us, they gon' have to come get us! I-swear-to-GOD!"

Mula said, "Bless His name." Hood dropped the duffel bag in front of us.

She said, "Our repertoire. Dig in, ladies."

Mula grabbed her 9's. Staring at 'em in admiration as she held them up, she said, "Chanteuses! On my birthday!" she smiled, clicking the barrels together. The club was empty. I'd just grabbed a Mac, when we heard shots ringing outside. While the rest of the crew grabbed their weapons, the doors swung open. Mula and Hood immediately reacted, ready to squeeze them hammers at the dark figures that came through the entrance. We'd all pointed our weapons in their direction.

The melodramatic-like moment is forever imprinted in my mind. Hood stopped us. "Waaaait!" she stretched her arms out, stepping in front of us. "Y'all, don't shoot! Be easy!" We were relieved to see that it was the twins that had walked through those doors. That's when we heard the news. It was true.

Moo said, "That was Action Sweets and Lue saw!" Hood didn't wanna hear it.

She said, "Boy, hush yo' mouth!" Like all of us, she was shocked!

Lue said, "Told y'all asses!" Bri couldn't believe it. She was cursing herself; all she kept saying was, "Fuck!" over and over again. She said, "I thought, I thought I—"

Moo said, "We'll talk about that later. Let's go!"

Mula said, looking back, "Hood, you get the money!"

"Yeah, I got it! Bring yo ass on here!" Hood replied. I had a Mac .90 in one hand, and my Giuseppe Zanotti pumps in the other. When we got outside, a hail of bullets flew our way as we were herded inside the back of a black Yukon parked directly in front of the exit with the rear doors open. We dove in, as 3 Chambers yoked back, giving us cover. But, bullets were still pinging off, and penetrating the SUV. We could actually hear them bitches whizzin' through.

Doe yelled, "Jilla, drive this mutha-fucka nigga!"

Gok! Gok-Gok-Gok! Gok-Gok-Gok-Gok! Gok-Gok-Gok! Goko-Goko-Goko-Goko-Goko!

They were bussin' somethin' heavy at us! Hood's crazy ass tried to raise up and shoot back, but Moo wasn't having it.

"Girl! Getcho ass down! What the-fuck you think you doin'!"

He pushed her back down, covering her body with his own. We fishtailed out the parking lot. I thought all of our asses were about to die! But, we made it.

Chapter 4

Hood

Shit, we came down! I had my red Tadashi Shoji dress on! My *Love Affair* diamonds! I'm runnin' around hosting this party with my social smile on! All the while, we slippin'! Hell n'all! I couldn't believe it! We'd gone to this nigga's funeral! I gotta call a spade a spade though. The cameo Action pulled that night showed his valor. What we had to do now, was get at him before he got back at us. Finding him was the problem. I mean, how do you find a dead nigga? I'd always thought their bones lay in cemeteries, while their souls lingered somewhere between Heaven or Hell. I guess I was wrong. He wasn't at the cemetery where he should've been, so it's time for his accolade. All the shots they'd sent! Aw, he deserved it. No doubt. Since he was on his J.D.'s revenge shit and wanted to see us, we couldn't leave him dissatisfied. Now could we? Shit, I was with it! But, there were others that weren't so supple about the situation. Especially the twins. They'd taken us to another one of their spots and went in on us. We'd fucked up *again*, so they had every right.

"You can't just double tap the head! You gotta tap the chest too!" Moo scolded Brianna. Disappointed and stressed, she was plunked down in a chair, fingers to her temples. I'd fired up a joint, and it had me coughing up my lungs! It hit me! And, hard!

"Oh..." Bri murmured. I couldn't help it. I let out this shrill burst of laughter, smoke exploding from my mouth.

"*Blaa-haa-ha-ha-haaa*!" everybody paused.

Doe said, "Tasha, what the fuck is so damn funny!" His face was all crumpled up. I hit that shit again.

Holding in my smoke, in a strained voice, I said: "We've been duped, fooled, bamboozled. The nigga Action ain't dead, huh?" I blew that shit out. "Y'all sure?" I questioned.

Moo said, "Nah, we ain't sure. I looked right at his ass! Who else gon' be shootin' at'chall like that!"

Bri looked up at me. Her eyes were smeared with tears, causing her makeup to run. I'd learned a true lesson early on. My momma always told me, the truth comes from kids, a drunken tongue, and those that didn't geh no fuck. My sistah was feeling real small at that moment as she looked at me in anticipation. She just stared malevolently. I knew she hated a stalemate.

I said, "Bri, it ain't shit. We just gon' get out here and kill this bitch for real." I smiled.

Doe said, "Yo' ass in this muthfucka sniggering! What if we wouldn't have made it to y'all asses in time!" I raised my eyebrows and shrugged. Resting my elbow on the table in thought, I rolled the joint in between my index finger and my thumb.

I said, "If we—"

"We would've shot it out! Hood, pass that shit!" Mula overrode. I passed her some. Smacking my lips, I had cotton mouth.

"Anybody seen his bitch?" Doe asked, looking pointedly at his watch. It was just a little past 3:00 a.m.

Sweets said, "Zoi? Yeah, she be around. She fuckin' with that nigga that call it for 2-7 now, ain't she?"

"Who? Jerry?" Moo asked omniously.

Mula said, "Yuuuup! I did see her drivin' his Benz! Her lil' triflin' ass." She frowned.

Moo said, "Well, there it is. We find his bitch and that baby, we find Action."

I said, "Oh, she ain't hard to find. I think she still stayin' in that same house. Matter of fact, I'm sure of it. And, whatchu mean "we"? We got this nigga."

Chapter 5

King SoVee
(A Day Prior)

As I stepped off the elevator at the Hilton, I was greeted by one of my old running buddies, Weight. We hadn't seen one another since we were doing time upstate in the Bay.

"King! Is that you, nigga!" Weight greeted me.

"Wasup, boy! Haaa! When you get out, nigga?" I asked, as we embraced each other with a handshake and a hug. "Look atchu! My boy, you done got big!"

"You know we gotta take care of ourselves." Weight smiled.

He said, "I've been out a few months now."

"Suit and tie? You lookin' like a businessman! What's this around ya neck?" I asked.

"Dog, you ain't heard? I'm doing it different now. I gave my life to Christ. No more street shit. I gave them people too much time. This here is an all access pass for a lil' concert tomorrow night over on Wisconsin. I'm helping my niggaz promote it. You ain't goin'?"

"Shit, I ain't heard nothin' about it," I replied.

"If you didn't know about it, that means we're not doing our jobs." He shook his head. "R.O.B. and R.O.S. gotta step our game up a notch or two."

"Aw n'all, I've been out of town for the past six or seven months. What's R.O.B. and R.O.S.?" I asked. "I've definitely been seeing it posted throughout the city."

"*Remembering Our Brothers* and *Remembering Our Sisters* are both my creations. They're nonprofit organizations for the kids, to the old timers. From prison, to those who've passed away as well. We trying to reach any and every neighborhood. You need us, we're there. You got kids, right? Send 'em to the center. Well, check it out. You got a minute?" he asked, setting his briefcase on the floor in the middle of the hallway, popping its locks. Opening it, he grabbed two handfuls of flyers and tickets. He closed the briefcase and stood up.

"Here you go," he said, handing me everything. "All that's free. All I ask is that wherever you stop between now and tomorrow night, is that you kindly drop a few of those flyers. That's at least twenty tickets. All access, and they're going for two hundred dollars each. Since we go back, that's you."

"Aw, n'all. I can't—" I shook my head.

"Them you, King."

"Damn, all these people gon' be there?" I asked, looking at the star-studded laminated passes.

"Hell yeah! It's being hosted by PYT. See there? Look, that's them at the bottom. They bad, ain't they?" He pressed the elevator's call button.

"Indeed. And you say this is tomorrow night?"

"Fa-sho." Reaching inside his jacket, he said, "Here, take my business card. It has my home and my work number on there. We do everything from concerts, camping trips for the kids, lunches in the summer, dinners at the church to group home for the elderly. I gotta run though. I'm late going to see this punk-ass P.O. as it is." He stepped into the elevator, extending his card to me.

I was still staring at the access passes.

"King!" He got my attention.

"Aw shit, my bad. Yeah-yeah-yeah. I hear you, and I'm there." I grabbed the card from between his fingers. We shook firmly. I said, "I appreciate this."

"Anytime. You already know." He smiled. "Don't forget about us now. Drop 'em wherever you head. There's also a few other things I wanna holla at you about. Call me!" The elevator doors began to close.

"I gotchu!" I replied.

"I heard about Rock and 'A'! I'm sorry. Until the storm!" Weight saluted me.

"Until the storm, my nigga!" I returned the gesture as the doors closed completely.

Chapter 6

Blood of my Brother

Walking the hall, I stopped at Room 3064. I could finally put faces to the names I'd been hearing so much about. As I swiped my key card, entering the room I was still staring at what I'd just received. Sinister impulses arose as I thought of Rock. My eyes blurred. I had murder in my heart. My pace quickened as I made into the sleeping area of the posh Presidential suite. I tapped lightly on the door that led inside the guestroom. I then walked towards the window, dropping everything on the delicate Chippendale desktop. As I looked over the city, I cuffed my hands behind my back. Action stuck his head out of the guestroom door.

"What up?" he asked, looking across the room at my back.

"I know y'all ain't still in there fuckin'. Put somethin' on real quick, and come holla at me. It's major."

"A'ight, give me a second." Hearing the eagerness in my voice, he threw his pants on and stepped out, pulling the door all the way closed behind him. He and Shasta had been going at it all night. He was tired.

"A'ight, what up?" he asked. But, ashamed of my tears, I didn't turn to greet him.

I said, "I guess we flew in just in time. What an irony."

"What? What's on your mind?" he asked in confusion.

"They're in celebration of y'all death, my nigga. Take a look at that shit." Turning to face him, I nodded towards the desk.

His face wrinkled in disgust as he read and spotted his old acquaintance and her friends. I imagined every muscle in his body tightened, and his hands began to sweat, as mine did.

"3C Entertainment, huh? Forever Music Presents? We in there, King. Let's make sure this party serves its purpose."

"You muthafuckin' right! For the blood of my brother!" I know he felt my pain.

He said, "I see they're spending my money. And well. Where you get all this from?"

"You wouldn't believe it. Weight."

"Weight, that nigga out?" he asked in disbelief.

"Yeah. Say he been out for a few months now. I ran into him on this very floor when I was getting off the elevator."

"What the fuck was he doing here?"

"I don't know. I didn't ask. I reckon he was gettin' him some pussy. But, he say he chillin'. He's a businessman now. Straight and narrow. At least that's what he say."

"Bullshit." Action frowned. "That nigga a killa. And always will be."

Chapter 7

Action

Brianna punk-ass was so preoccupied up under that signin' ass nigga, she ain't even recognize me. If I'd had a buck-fifty I could've slit her muthafuckin' throat! I was standing right next to her. When the twins pulled up, one of 'em recognized me right away. My funeral was held and everything. I know they gotta be wondering how the fuck I'm still alive. Well, that's what money do. O.G. knew how they'd left me, that somebody wanted her son dead! And they weren't bullshittin'. It's either by fate, or the grace of God, that I'm still breathing. Her ties as a Mason go a long way. Somebody up the chain owed her some major favors. People in high places. The things they can do! On paper, I'm officially deceased. After multiple surgeries on my brain, face and skull, I'm looking halfway decent. The back, and top of my head has this big mound on it. It's where the surgeons had to reconstruct and place steel in my shit. My face is somewhat contorted, so I grew my beard all the way out. Mustache too. I guess the doctors did the best they could. Ma-Duke begged me to just split, but I can't let these lil' bitches get off on me like that! Nah, I'm on that ass! We just let a few drums go at 'em, but they got away. I'm pissed!

***

"Flacko! I had'em blocked in from this side! How the fuck you let'em get past you?"

"I had to reload, nigga! You see all them niggaz I had to keep off your ass!" he replied.

"That was them 3C niggaz, huh?" SoVee questioned.

"Yeah, that was them!"

"Just get y'all ass in the car! The police comin'!" Flacko yelled from across the street. We jumped in and got up outta there. We hit Wells speedin'.

Since Eric Charlse no longer exists, I gotta be careful in who I fuck with. The only people that knew I was alive, besides those responsible for saving me, were my momma, Flacko, SoVee, and my old love—Shasta. Now, all that has changed. King SoVee is Rock's brother. Since the bitch was true to her word in making sure my nigga didn't make it, I figured he'd be a good asset in getting vengeance against these nefarious hoes. Zoi has no idea I'm still alive. All her crocodile tears ain't mean shit, anyway. You'd think she would've taken a few months to grieve if she truly loved me. But, nah. According to my momma, she'd moved a nigga in our house four months after they'd supposedly put me in the ground. It's true. I've been watching them go about life the past few days as if I've been gone twenty years. Nigga driving my cars, picking my son up from daycare and everything. That's what I get for puttin' shit in her name. She's got it all. My son, the deeds to all the houses as well. She'd been blessed with $750,000 I had on me for my life insurance, plus the million I told momz to give her if anything were to happen to me. Duke was hesitant in giving her the money at first. But, believing Zoi's love for me was genuine, she wanted to look out for her and my shorty. She dropped the bread, feeling me and Zoi were going to be together anyway. After seeing this shit with my own eyes, there's no way that's even possible. See, I know this nigga she fuckin' with. He 2-7, and got some paper of his own.

It makes a nigga wonder, *had they been fuckin' around all along*? That's something I'd definitely have to dig into. When you fuck a nigga's bitch, sometimes it's deemed cool in the hood. But, to me that's until a man becomes one with her and calls her his wife. After that, all that don't-blame-the-player shit goes out the window. You cross that line, you should expect bodily harm. Why? Because you've welcomed it. It takes two, so that goes for both parties. I've got no problem with her moving on. I'm supposedly dead. How she done is fucked up, but life goes on. Right now, the only thing saving her is my son. Him, and confirmation on how long this shit's been going on. I'll get to the bottom of it though. I think I know exactly where to find all my answers too.

Chapter 8

Love Thy Enemy
—Goldie

The stench of mildew fills my nostrils. I've regained consciousness, which gives me hope, since I'm still alive. Freezing and in pain, my body is shivering. The basement I'm being held in is cold and wet. Most of the blood that covers my naked frame has dried and hardened against my skin. Bound to a steel chair with chains and padlocks, my mouth is covered with duct-tape. My head is throbbing from the savage beatings I'd received, as I search the darkness for a glimmer of light. For what seems like hundreds of hours, there was nothing. Suddenly, I hear what sounds like a door opening and closing. Voices, as well as footsteps, can be heard coming from the floor directly above me. Fear of the unknown weighs heavily upon my soul. A light came on, sending a pained surprise to my brain that's so excruciating that I can't bear to keep my eyes open. I can hear the distinctive clatter of metal, and the thuds of their footsteps as they came down the stairs. Flickering my eyes momentarily, I caught a glimpse of two figures dressed in black. One looked to be carrying something heavy. Recognizing their voices as they spoke, there's no longer a question in my mind as to who stands before me. My fears are warranted.

"Ooh-wee! It's snowin' harder than a muthafucka out there!" Moo kicked the grey brick wall, shaking the snow from his boots. Doe laughed.

"Ha-haaa! Look at this nigga. Yetta and Wintress got 'em down here freezin' his lil' nuts off."

"Mm-hmm, fuck 'em. Serves that ass right. Goldie, you still my nigga? You still A.T.K., ain'tchu!" Moo chuckled. Doe grabbed me by my face and raised my head.

He said, "Yeah, we still niggaz. Even though you sent the other side to kill me." He muffed me. My eyes bucked at his statement's truth. I tried to speak, but the adhesive had my lips sealed tight.

"Mm-hmm-mm-mmm!" I grunted.

"I know! I knooow. Calm down, Gold. Look atchu. You got me shaking my damn head, boy. We shouldn't even be here. Not like this, anyway. But, I know what you gotta be thinking. I mean, all these niggaz comin' down here beating on you like you a runaway slave. The least we could do is come and check on you!" Doe said dryly, as he pulled the latex gloves over his hands.

"Kunta!" Moo sighed. "Damn, how did it come to this?" He sat the toolbox down and opened it. Rifling through the tools, he fished out a claw hammer. He then pulled his gun from the waistline of his pants. He said, "Look at me, nigga!" He held his gaze until our eyes finally met.

"Which tool do you prefer? *Ms. Complication?*" He held up the hammer. "Or *Ms. Simplicity* here?" He smiled, brandishing the .9mm.

Doe said, "Fuck that, I'ma choose!" He snatched the hammer and whacked me in my right kneecap, causing me to let out a muffled howl.

"Mmmmmmm!" I grimaced.

"Shh-shhh-shhhh. Not yet, my nigga," Doe whispered in my ear. "We're just gettin' started." He whacked me again, shattering my other knee. Tucking his gun, Moo snatched the tape from my swollen lips.

"Ahhhhhhhh!" I yelped. "I-I- sti-still ain't go-got shit for you bi-bitch ass niggaz!" I spat.

"Bitch ass niggaz? Whoa! You need a minute?" Moo asked, as Doe handed him the hammer. "Let me know. 'Cause, you know I got a few questions for you. You-you ready?" he taunted. "You gon' tell us everything we wanna know, cuz." He sneered, swinging the hammer.

They'd taken turns beating me for hours, but I didn't budge. This is where betrayal landed me. I'm hurt bad, and they're frustrated. The bitter taste of blood coated my tongue as Doe stood   before me with his finger curled inside the trigger loop. He was about to apply pressure, taking me out of my misery when Moo grabbed his arm.

"Hold on, bruh. That'll be too lenient on 'em. Let me work him some more. He'll talk."

"Uh-un." Doe shook his head. "You may be right, but this nigga must think we playin'. I'ma gon' take care of him." He lowered his gun and winked at his brother. "This for me and Jah. You get up outta here. Be sure to make yourself seen. Tell Jilla, I said an hour." He wiped a lone tear away.

"Yo, you sure?" Moo questioned.

"Yeah, you sure?" I scoffed, spitting blood as I spoke.

"I'm positive." Doe tucked the .45 in his jeans at the small of his back and pulled his sweater over it.

"A'ight." Moo threw his hoodie over his head. "I'm out."

"One!" Doe yelled, as Moo climbed the stairs.

"I gotchu." Moo replied.

Chapter 9

Doe

Beatin' the truth out of Goldie should've been something I enjoyed. But every blow that struck him also struck the core within me. My mind kept flashing back to all our childhood memories. Somehow, gettin' involved in the streets had changed it all. We'd come to the point of no return. The guns came out, so mercy was no longer an option. If you ever had to fuck a nigga up that you love, then maybe you know how I feel. Him being the first, who's to say he'll be the last. Tomorrow would have to worry about itself.

In punishment and promise, he'd finally given it all up: The stash he kept at his bitch Kecha crib. The codes niggaz used at the spot on Atkinson. He also revealed how to catch up to the nigga—Po Kelly. It turns out Po, and a bunch of the older Burleigh niggaz, decided to get on some renegade shit after J.L.'s cranium literally rolled. I guess the old heads can't find it in themselves to honor Lil' Zoo's right of passage as their next king. This brought on a war between the old and the new. This explains why cats from over that way been gettin' stunk on a regular again. I needed no reminder that Ross and Po are two of the deadliest niggaz the city has ever seen. I've witnessed Po's flames, though he'd failed to finish me. Personally, I had nothing against Ross, until I learned through this nigga's confessions that he had a hand in the slaughter of my two lil' niggaaz—Too Deep and Joshie. Without a doubt, both of them niggaz gon' have to see me.

Goldie told me everything I needed to know. And though I promised Goldie I'd let him go if he left the state, it was a promise I knew I wouldn't be able to keep when I'd made it. I had a job to do. So, after he finished, I grabbed the hammer and walked up on 'em again.

"Please, please, *pleeease* don't kill me!"

He begged for his life, but I went to work. When Jilla got there, I'd already had him wrapped in plastic. Leave it to this nigga to show up high. Eyes all low and shit.

He said: "Damn, nigga! You've done this shit before, haven't you?" He studied my expression as we lifted the body. I shook my head.

"Nah." I lied. "This is the most time I've ever spent with the dead right here. You higher than a muthafucka, ain'tchu?" I laughed. He grinned.

"I chiefed a lil' sun-thin sun-thin. Why? You could've smoked with me, but you spending time with the deceased, huh? I can tell by the look on yo' face that you didn't like it. Did he give up?"

"Did he? It went exactly as I said it would. He said he got about a mil and a half at Kecha crib that she don't even know about."

"You bullshittin'! Where at? We put alligator bumps and lumps on this nigga, and he wouldn't tell us nothin'!"

"In the attic." I smiled.

"Well, it look like we gon' have to pay Kecha lil' ass a visit then, huh?"

"You muthafuckin' right."

"You don't plan on—you know?"

"What?"

"Spending no time with her. I wanna hit that."

"Hell naw. Kecha cool. You got some more weed, nigga?"

After we'd stuffed Goldie in the trunk and closed it, he pulled out a half ounce of that burma.

"Yea-yup! You know it!" he replied, lookin' like Cube from his N.W.A. days.

With his love for the weed, Jilla mean-mugged me and said, "Whatchu wanna do?" He knew I rarely smoked.

"Let's go get the girls so they can clean up all this blood and shit. Then we can get our drink and our smoke on. I need it after all this shit." As I looped around the passenger side, he said, "You really loved this nigga, huh?" I paused. Peering at him over the roof of the Lac, I gave little thought to his question. There was no need.

"Of course I did," I replied.

"God said, love thy enemy." Jilla shook his head. He jumped in, slammed the door and started the car. I got in. After closing my door, I looked at him.

I said, "You know what?"

"Wasup?" We'd pulled off, heading down the alleyway.

I said, "At first, I didn't see how that shit was even possible."

Chapter 10

Taken
—Zoi

I just got my hair done, and it's just my luck that I'm caught in the middle of a thunderstorm. It's pouring rain out here. As lightning does its staccato dance across the sky, the windshield wipers on my BMW are working overtime. Pulling in my driveway, I had my hands full. EJ is fast asleep, and since I just left the grocery store, I've got a lot of bags to unload as well. I've been meaning to have an automatic garage door opener installed, but I've been putting it off for the longest. Now, I wish I'd chosen differently. I gotta get out, unlock the garage, and lift the door! Sliding off track at times, it can be stubbornly irritating.

I turned the car off, and hopped out, arms flailing as I tried my best to dodge the rain drops. I'd reached the door, stuck the key in, twisted the knob and lifted with all my might! It didn't budge. "Shit!" I cursed, as I continued to pull. It finally opened. Running back to the car, I got in and pulled it inside. Before turning off the ignition, I popped the trunk. Unlocking his seatbelt, I grabbed Eric junior from his car seat. He hadn't heard a thing. His eyes fluttered, but he'd fallen back to sleep in my arms.

"Wake up, boy! With your heavy self." I smiled at my stank-a-booty as I carried him inside and laid him on the couch. I then headed back out to get the groceries. Steak and lobster were on tonight's menu. I was unloading the first bag from the trunk of my car when I was startled by masked intruders.

I was grabbed from behind as I attempted to scream. A black leather glove tightly covering my mouth and my nose, I couldn't breathe. I kicked and struggled in a ghastly attempt to break free. A gun was then pressed against my head. Another was aimed squarely at my chest.

"Bitch, be still! You bet' not scream. Go get the baby! Take 'em!" It's a hardened voice I recognized, and will never forget. I can't believe this shit is happening to us again. Three assailants ran in my home, guns up.

"Scream, and you's a dead bitch. You hear me? You got it?" With strain in my face and horror in my eyes, I nodded in agreement. I was flung to the garage's concrete floor, as I gasped for air. I was then zip-tied and duct-taped. "Throw the bags out and put her ass in the trunk!" the voice commanded. Consumed by terror, my mouth is shaking and my body is quivering as I'm lifted to my feet, and then shoved in the trunk. My dreadful cries couldn't be heard. With duct-tape wrapped around my head, covering my eyes and mouth, I've got two senses left. I can no longer see the shadowy figures in their skiwear, nor the guns, but I knew they were there. I could hear and feel their presence. My life and my son's were in peril! The trunk slammed, trapping me inside.

I heard, "Y'all got'em! Go 'head, we right behind y'all! I then heard and felt the weight of them getting in, and the doors slamming. My car started.

I could feel it being slowly backed out of the garage. I then heard gunfire, causing my body to skitter and jolt with every blast.

***

Bri

"What the—" Hood hit the breaks, and we all looked back.

Lah! Lah! Laow! Shots rang out.

Bak! Bak! Bak-Bak-Bak! "Hood, pull out!" Mula yelled, dumpin' her 9's.

Boom! Boom! Boom-Boom-Boom!

"It's Action!" Sweets shouted over the shotty's blaze as Cyn dove in the van with EJ. He was crying for his mother. They'd burst their guns at Action, but it did little in slowing him down.

Lah-Lah-Lah! He sent rounds wildly as he sped up the block.

Bak-Bak! Bak-Bak-Bak-Bak-Bak-Bak! Mula let go. Again, Sweets followed.

Booom! Boooom! Cyn was in the driver seat of the van.

"Let's gooooo!" she called out of the window. *Bak-Bak!* Mula got off two more before they jumped in the van.

Hood looked at me and Lue. She said, "Dammit! Stay down, and just hold on!" She gunned the Beamer. Flooring it, the engine stood up from zero to sixty. Seeing us flying down the driveway backwards, Action sent two shots in our direction, shattering the back window.

"Ahhhhhh!" Hood screamed in agony. She clipped the ass end of the coupé as Action tried to give chase to the van. The collision caused his car to spin, jump the curb and hit a light pole. The BMW spun a full three-hundred-sixty degrees and hit a tree. Hood was hit. She'd also banged her head on the steering wheel, and was unconscious.

Chapter 11

Cyn

As we raced up Fon Du Lac, Mula searched the traffic behind us.

"Cyn!" she called out to me from the back. "Bitch, I don't see 'em! We gotta go back!" she yelled.

"Ma-maaaaa!" EJ cried at the top of his lungs. The gunfire had him petrified.

"Cyn, I know you hear me! Sweets, shut that little muthafucka up! Cyn, turn this bitch around!" Mula demanded.

"He's already blindfolded, hell! What else you want me to do?" Sweets asked in frustration.

"I-I don't know! Put somethin' in his mouth!" She threw her the duct-tape.

"Cyn!"

"But Hood said—" I pled with my eyes, looking at her through the rearview as she rushed to the front.

"Fuck that, move! I'm drivin'! We can't leave 'em! Something not right!" She took the wheel as I slid into the passenger seat. The tires screeched as she hit the brakes and swung the wheel, heading back.

***

Bri

"Hood! Hood, we—we gotta go!" I shook her. "She—she's hit! Lue, cover us!" Lue jumped out the back. And with no hesitation, she ran around the car, sending rounds into the money green Benz. There was no movement. I hopped out and ran around to the driver's side and opened the door. Hood was awake, but dizzy and in pain.

"Oomph!" she moaned. She was bleeding bad as I dragged her out the car.

"Come on, Hood, walk with me! We gotta move!

Masked up, guns in hand, it was raining cats and dogs and we were stranded.

My head was spinning. I yelled, "Fuck, Lue-Lue! We need a car!"

"I know, bitch! I knooow!" Lue yelled back at me in despair, clutching two Macs.

Cold and drenched, we slowly moved up the block. Holding the wound in her neck, Hood was using me as a crutch.

With Hood wounded and weak, we didn't have her cosmic thinking. To our relief, looking up the block, Lue spotted the van we'd stolen earlier. Before Mula even tapped the breaks, the conversion door slid open.

"Come on!" Mula yelled.

"She hit?" Sweets asked.

"Yeah," I replied. Help us get her in. We jumped in, and Mula smashed out.

***

Action

When I came to, I got out and ran up on the BMW, but they were gone. Hearing loud thuds coming from the trunk, I knew it had to be Zoi. I thought about letting her ass out, but hearing sirens approaching in the distance, I decided against it. I hopped back in the Benz, hoping it was still drivable. It was, and I got up outta there. *Bitches got away with my son*! I thought to myself.

***

Cyn

The tires hissed across the wet pavement as we sped through the city. Hood was stretched out across the back seat with her head lying in Lue's lap. The blood she was losing had her mask sticking to her skin. It was thick, like syrup. She was in pain, though she had nothing but fury in her splendid eyes. Bri was trying to take her mask off so we could see the wound, but she was giving her a hard time. She'd twisted, turned and pushed her hand away.

"Hood, stop! Hold her, Lue!" Bri pled.

"I can't! Somebody help me!" Lue was struggling. Sweets moved in to help, and Hood threw a kick at her. Dodging it, she managed to grab her legs.

"We gotta get her to a hospital!" I cried.

"No. No hospitals. Take me to Tip's. Call my brothers." She grimaced faintly, in a sandpapery voice. We were scared!

"Hood, move your hand, bitch!" Mula barked in tears. "Stop being so damn bullheaded!" she snarled ferociously like a she-wolf. There was no warmth in her gaze. Hood had to be strong for us. Her dawgs. She drew the courage and finally gave in. Moving her hand, she let Bri peel off the mask. She was sweaty, wet, and breathing heavily.

"There you go. S-s-s-s-s!" Bri hissed, as if she was feeling her pain. "Let me see. Just hold still. It's gon' be okay." She held her hand, giving her a complacent nod as she took the mask off.

Chapter 12

Gina

I heard the code for shots fired. It was in the air, so I rushed to the scene. I'd recognized the address from a case that was taken from me roughly a year and a half ago. Something has always bothered me about that one. Call me blind to darkness, but I ain't nobody's fool. Last time I was at the location, somebody was tying to sell me death. I'd gone expecting to find a body, but when I got there, there wasn't one on the scene. There wasn't much else for me to go on either. There were two bloody pillows laying there on the floor of the living room. Someone had clearly used them to muffle the sound of gunfire. Both pillows had muzzle burns which told me that much. I found the pool of blood on the floor to be the most peculiar. It had coagulated. That meant it would've had to be there from anywhere between fifteen and twenty minutes, at least! I'd arrived in less than seven once I'd gotten the call. But, when I got there, I was told the victim, a Mr. Eric Charlse had been pronounced dead and the coroner had already taken the body. I snapped! I'm wondering why the fuck they'd even bothered calling me in the first place. I'd brushed it off as some hatin' shit going on downtown, and let it go. Then, while I'm questioning the surviving home's owner, my lieutenant pops up! He's telling me to just head home and take the day off. Talking about my attitude, he claimed that he'd gotten a call saying I was on the scene cursing everybody out. I still ponder on that to this day. Who could've made the call? I'd cussed, like a sailor and some more shit. Hell yeah, sure did. But rather than trying to figure it out, I just left. That wouldn't be the case today though. I hope. It wasn't a Code 3, but I had to see what was going on over there. What was up on Silver Spring this time?

I pulled up to see a black BMW wrapped around a tree. I'd took notice that the front windshield and the back window were both shattered. There was also a bullet hole in the back quarter panel on the right side of the vehicle. Officers on the scene were having a hard time containing Mrs. Love-Charlse. I jumped out of my car, hand on my weapon. She was acting out! Lookin' all wild, her clothes all dishevelled. She had a piece of duct-tape in her hair, and some stuck to her face. The officers that arrived before me had their weapons drawn as she paced back and forth in the middle of the street.

"Ma'am! We're going to need you to calm down! We're here to help!" a fellow officer shouted. I'm thinking, *why is this trunk open*? I also notice zip ties on the ground as I surveyed the scene.

She yelled, "They got my bay-beee! They got my sonnn! Are y'all even listening to meeee! Y'all need to—"

Situation read! I took my hand off my gun, and stepped forward.

"You're in the line! Officer, you're in the line of fire!" one of the other Cops yelled. I waved him off.

"Chill! Everybody, chill! Zoi, hi baby! I'm Gina Burke from Homicide. You remember me? I—"

"Ms. Burke, these muuthafuckaz took my baby!"

"Who! Mrs. Love-Charlse, who took your baby?" I asked. "Do you mean he's been kidnapped?"

"Ye-yeaaah! They got'eeem!" she cried, jumping up and down.

"You need to calm down! Come down to the station and—" another officer yelled from behind me. They were new transfers to the precinct, so I wasn't familiar with them at all.

"I ain't goin' to no mutha-fuckin' station! For what, huh!"

"Excuse me, what's your name?" I turned and asked his dumb ass!

"Canup! Detective Canup!" he replied, ready to shoot this woman.

"Canup, where was this young lady when you arrived!"

"She was in the trunk," he replied.

"I figured that much. Lower your weapon and let me talk to her! Somebody get the

FBI out here! Do it! Do it right now!" I commanded. "Every second counts!"

"Who and the hell do you think—"

"Canup! She's not the threat! Just stand down and let me talk to her! She knows me!" I turned my attention back towards the victim. "Zoi! Zoi, it's bad out here. How about we head inside and you can tell me what's going on? You can tell me everything that happened. What's your son's name?" I asked, snapping my fingers as she paced. Then it hit me. "Eric! Little Eric, y'all call him EJ, right? This is the only way we'll find him."

Nodding, she said, "Yeah." She paused and put her hands on her knees, trying to catch her breath. "We—we call'em EJ."

"This is how it works. This is how we find him. You need to tell us everything, okay? Come on." I eased in, grabbing her gently by her arm. She broke down in tears as I led her inside. Canup followed, which was good. He could write the report, because I don't do'em. As we walked in, I heard him yell, "What are you guys standing around for! You heard her! Let's get the FBI out here!"

Sitting in he living room, she filled us in on what occurred by her account. I was having a hard time believing her story because she was all over the place. At Keyara's getting her hair done. At Kohl's doing her grocery shopping. Then, she's in her garage with guns in her face.

First, she said it was six dudes before switching her statement to it being five men and a female. What really made me feel like she was either crazy or losing her damn mind was when she said it may have been three men and three women. She said, she could have sworn she'd heard a female yell: "Hood, pull out!" Or, "Hood, get out!" Multiple gunshots were fired. We knew that to be true. We had the casings and shotgun shells. She said she also heard a female mention Action, one of whom is her late husband. He'd been deceased for a little over a year. Even crazier, she'd said she could've sworn she'd seen him sitting down the streets from here last week. But, she'd brushed it off as having an episode of her mind playing tricks on her. She seemed to really miss him, at first. When I'd asked her if she was currently dating anyone? To my surprise, she'd told me yes. She said his name was Jerry Walker. It's a name I'm quite familiar with, being he's one of the city's biggest drug dealers. I figured this could have everything to do with him, and not her. I asked if she knew where he was? She stated that he was out of town, but she was expecting him later on tonight. I also asked her if she knew anyone that would want to hurt her, or her child. She said, no. That's when Canup's partner stepped in.

He said, "Excuse me for a sec, guys. Cap, I've got great news! The FBI is in route. I also just spoke to a 63-year-old veteran, Mr. Burlap, that lives across the street! He was absolutely astounded. He said he saw everything! And boy, does he know his stuff!" he flipped out his notepad. "Let's see. He says he heard gunshots at approximately fourteen-hundred hours, so he looks out of his window. He observes two individuals shooting southbound up the block, which is this way." he pointed towards our left.

Canup said, "I know which way it is! Just get on with it, will ya!" He then looks at me and says, "Rookies." I shrugged.

"Okay," the new boot said nervously. He said: "He says— Wait a minute. Okay, here it is. He says there were three males in all black wearing ski masks outside the home. One had a shotgun with the stock as well as the barrel sawed off. The other one involved in the shooting was discharging two

.9 mills! This guy could tell the make of each weapon by the sound. I find that amazing! He says we should find tactical rounds from the shotgun, and he was right! Amazing, don't you think? I mean, with the rain and all. Uh, anyway, he says there was a third carrying a kid. That one was carrying a Mac-10 or 11. Says he couldn't say for sure because it wasn't fired. They'd driven off in a blue van. GMC, a big one." He flipped the page. "Okay, after they drove off, a green Mercedes gives chase! Or, tries to. The BMW outside that's usually driven by Mrs. Love-Charlse here comes down the driveway like a bat outta hell, when the black guy in the Benz lets two go into the BMW! This would be just before the BMW crashes into him, causing them both to crash."

"He says the Benz was actually on his front lawn after it bounced off the light pole. He stated one of the three occupants that were in the BMW exits the rear driver's side door and fires eighty to a hundred rounds from two semiautomatic weapons, he believes to Mac-10 in caliber. He says the drivers of both vehicles seemed pretty banged up. He believes the driver of the BMW was injured. Wounded by gunfire or the collision itself. We did find some blood. Burlap says, the assailants made it up the block some ways before the blue GMC doubled back and picked them up."

I was starting to believe! Now that there was a second witness. I had to be sure I wasn't being sold a kidnapping, being I was served death cold at this very address.

"You done?" Canup asked.

"I think so. No, wait! There's actually one more thing I found interesting. The—the guy! The one that fled in the Benz. He says, this guy was actually about the same height and build as the guy that used to live here with Mrs. Love-Charlse just over a year ago. Says he got a pretty good look at him."

"Okay, now are you done?" Canup asked, sounding a bit irritated.

"Yes'm" the rookie replied.

"Good work. Have a seat. Mrs. Love-Charlse, may I ask you a few questions? Canup asked.

"What was your son wearing when you saw him last? Do you have any recent photos of him?"

"Em-hmm." She stepped over to the China cabinet, opened it and grabbed a picture.

She said, "They didn't take his coat. He was wearing a blue, red and white Coca-Cola sweater, frosty Levi's, and some blue and white Reebok Pumps."

"How old is he now?" I asked.

"Twenty months," she replied as Canup handed me the photograph of baby EJ.

Chapter 13

FBI
Gina

"I'll take that." The FBI agents appeared like ghost! "We'll take it from here." One of them said, snatching the notes from Canup and the rookie. Then, another had the nerve to come take the picture of Lil' EJ from my ass. Rude bitches! Another began setting up a wire tap as we were relieved. When I left there, it really had me thinking. Who would've actually gone to that extreme? Shootin' up the block like that trying to save Eric Junior? The weapons being used had me in thought. *Nah, it's not their M.O.!* I thought to myself, as I paused at the red light taking a sip of my coffee, which was now cold as shit. I went home, cooked for me and my baby, then called Jamison and chewed his ear off all night about the case. Even though it wasn't mine, shit wasn't adding up!

I said, "Jamison, you know what!"

"What, Cakes?" he sighed dreadfully.

"I need to see that coroner's report on Eric Charlse."

He said, "So make the call."

I said, " Boy, you know that bitch don't fuck with me like that!" Kara is best friends with Jenna stank ass. So the coroner and the Medical Examiner be on some fuck Gina type shit. I said, "And you know me! I don't kiss no ass, period! I didn't attend the University! So, fuck them too!"

"He said, "I'll see what I can do," and hung up.

When I walked in the precinct the next morning, his ass was trying to be funny! Sitting his fat ass behind my desk with his feet all kicked up, smilin'.

I said, "What you doin' in my shit! You got a desk over there!"

He said, "Good morning. Why, if it isn't Burkey Cakes. Here, the coroner's report you requested." He picked the file up and handed it to me. "Of course I had to do a little carpet munching to get it, but what the hell." He smiled, as I grabbed the manilla folder.

I said, "Damn! I ain't tell you to go that far. Yo—You've got something stuck in your teeth. It looks like some hair." I smiled. "Is he in?" I walked towards our boss's dwelling in the station.

"He is," Jamison replied. I had a few unanswered questions about the morning Mr. Charlse was killed. I knocked on the door, then turned and yelled, "Jamison, stop leaning in my chair before you before you break it! Get out my shit!" I smiled.

Chapter 14

Lue

When we pulled up in front of Ms. Tippy's, we had to hurry up and pull Hood out so Mula could dump the van and burn it. Running in ahead of everybody, I'd interrupted Tip and her friend's game of Tonk as I fell in the back door. I was out of breath! And yeah, I ain't gonna lie. I was scared, a'ight!

"Ms. Tip! It—It's Hood! It's Tasha! Sh-she's—" Coming in behind me, Bri and Sweets carried her in, while Cyn dipped in the basement with Lil' EJ. All that could be heard were screams, as Hood collapsed on the kitchen floor, holding her mask against the wound in her neck.

"Tashaaaaaah! Oh my Godddd!" Tip rushed to her side. The slug had grazed her. It was still bleeding pretty bad. Plus, one side of her forehead was the size of a baseball.

"What-wha! What happened? Somebody call the ambulance!" Tippy yelled.

Hood said, "Nah, I'm a'ight, Tip. Just call Moo and Doe. Get me a steak or some ice or something." She rolled her body in pain, rocking her knees from side to side.

"What the hell you mean you all right! You bleedin'! And look atcho damn head! Who done jumped on you!" she questioned. "Let me see!" she said, grabbing the hand she held the bloody mask in.

The laceration stretched about three inches across the right side of her neck. Tippy insisted that she should go to the hospital to get some stitches, and make sure she didn't have a concussion. She said, "Girl, you might have blood on

47

the brain! You better take yo' ass to the emergency room!" But Hood asked her to give it some time, promising her that if the knot on her head didn't go down, she'd go to the doctor. When the twins got there, everything changed. Although she didn't want to, she had to swallow her pride. We needed help. Seeing their baby sister in the state she was in, we didn't have to ask. Within minutes, the house was full of 3C members and heavy arms. Shit, even Teague showed up, and we'd barely seen his ass. They were ready for war, but we had a situation on our hands. News of the kidnapping horrified and angered the residents of the community. Hundreds marched with banners and signs demanding EJ's return. While the police were looking in all the wrong directions, weeks went by. Since Zoi hadn't received a ransom demand, the FBI didn't hide the fact that they were deeply involved. What they didn't know was that through links in the streets, the twins had already spoken to Action. They didn't quite get the reaction they'd expected when they offered to exchange a life for a life. His bitch-ass told Moo and Doe to kill him! That's right. He told them to kill his son! He said he didn't give a fuck! The nigga said he'd make another one. It pissed me the fuck off! So, I decided to let the world in on his little secret.

Chapter 15

Weight

It was the night of the kidnapping. I'd laid down at 10:00 PM, but I couldn't sleep because my phone was ringing off the hook. I'd finally gotten up and answered it.

"Damn! Who dis?" I asked, groggily.

To my surprise, it was King at 4:30-ish in the muthafuckin' morning.

"Weight, this King SoVee. I need to holla atchu!"

"Okay, we can meet up to—"

"N'all, I need to holla atchu now. You hear about the lil' boy out on Silver Spring?"

"That somebody ran in that crib and snatched? Yeah, I heard about that. It's all over the news," I replied, sitting up.

He said, "That was Action's son, my nigga. You say you all about the kids, right?"

"Word, no doubt."

"Well, I need your help."

I was tired, but he'd reeled me in. Giving King my address, he came through. But, he wasn't alone as he'd said he'd be. He had company. It was Action! I couldn't believe it. I was stunned. A nigga that was supposed to be dead was standing in my living room. When King called, I thought he simply wanted R-O-B and R-O-S to assist him and the community's search, but he had other things in mind.

I said, "Son-of-ah! You're alive, huh? Come on in! Have a seat!" I offered them both, after firm handshakes. They took seats on the couch, and I'd sat across from them. Action didn't have much to say, so I took lead. As I explained how I thought our organization could aid them in the search, neither seemed too interested. They'd started asking questions about my nigga I'd done time in the Feds with. It didn't make sense to me. These cats and I had done our time together upstate. What did Teague and his family have to do with this? Not answering questions to their liking, shit got heated. Literally! I had a keen sense something was about to go down. I could just feel it. I was in my kitchen pouring the three of us some coffee, when I felt the cold steel press up against the back of my neck.

"Nigga, don't move unless I say so." Action got the drop on me. I was right. I hated I was right! I was unarmed. I didn't own a gun. I couldn't risk it, knowing myself. That other me. It was now a problem I'd have to face head on.

He said, "We gon' sit yo' ass down over here at the table." I gave a subtle nod. "King!" he called out.

SoVee walked in the kitchen. We just looked at each other. I'm sure he saw the disappointment of his betrayal all in my face. He shook his head as he walked towards me like I was in the wrong. Some homeboys these niggaz turned out to be.

He said, "It's a storm, Weight. I was hoping you'd be with me to ride through it. Now, I know you can tell me somethin'. Gon' sit. Sit down!" he commanded. I took a seat. I didn't have much of a choice. He said, "Keep that iron on him, 'A', until I can find something to tie him up with."

In his search of my house, he'd been in my bedroom. I knew because he'd returned with two of my leather belts, and two of my brand new neckties. They'd tied me to the chair as tight as they could, after making me strip down to my drawers. Walking over to the stove, Action said, "What we got here? Is this some chicken, or some fish grease you got over here?" He turned the eye on the stove on, and all the way up. The stove was ticking. I could see the yellow, orange and blue flames under the pot, as it ignited the grease I'd used to deep-fry some lake perch the night before. It wasn't long before I could hear the grease crackling, and begin to pop. Action hoe-ass laughed.

He said, "Aw, Weight, yo' ass gon' talk. Believe me. Where Teague lay his head at, nigga?"

Steeeezzz!

"Ahhhhhhhhhhhh!" this muthafucka took one of my big spoons and flung some of that hot ass grease across my back! "Ahhhhhhhhhhhhhhh! You biiiiitch-ass nigggah! You biiiiitch!" He'd hit me again. I'd rocked the chair so hard, it fell over with me in it. I was still holding my tongue though. They ain't like that.

King said, "Get his ass up!" When Action sat me up, I spit in his face.

"Fuck you niggaz!" I spat. Wiping the saliva from his face, Action was pissed!

He said, "Oh, you wanna act stupid!" He grabbed the pot and sat it on the floor. "We gone dip his feet off-in-this-shit! We'll see who the bitch is!" He'd sat the pot in front of my chair, King pulled the chair back, and slid me forward. I could feel the grease burning the bottom off my feet and my legs as it sizzled and leaped out the pot.

"I don't know! I don't know, got dammit! All I got is a number for the twins! I can call 'em!" I protested.

"All right, that's more like it!" King slid me back and away from the pot. He said, "What's the number, my nigga?" He grabbed the phone off the wall. I gave the number to him, and Action slapped me across my head with the pistol.

Chapter 16

Zoi

We've patrolled the city for weeks in search of direction. We'd posted missing persons flyers from here to Chicago, but my son is still nowhere to be found. The unmistakable feeling of hopelessness has begun to sink in. I haven't received a ransom demand, and in my eyes the FBI didn't have an inkling as to what was really going on. Though they've promised me that they'll find EJ, I know they're simply being optimistic. At times I felt like a suspect, and imprisoned in my own home. Though I've recited my story over and over, I was continuously and constantly asked to tell it to them again and again. They'd torn my house up from top to bottom in search of anything that would somehow implicate me. They'd found nothing. My dude, Jay, acting real funny. But I understand. He'd been detained for questioning. It took hours. He doesn't appreciate being under the scope, given the life he leads. It's not a good look. Now, they've gone. The FBI left, but all my lines are tapped just in case I get word from the kidnappers. Every time the phone rings, my heart flutters in desperation. Wondering if my baby is dead or alive! This time is no different as I ran from the kitchenette to answer it.

"Hell—hello?" I answered in a low voice.

"Zo, it's us, girl!" Saharah yelled.

"Zoi, bitch turn on the—" Oletta chimed in.

"Turn on the radio!" Timber overode. They'd hit me on a 3-way.

"Will y'all all stop trying to talk at the same damn time, please!"

Saharah said, "WNOV! Hurry up!"

"Why! What happened? I asked, moving feverishly towards my stereo. I felt like a piece of glass that was about to break! My being trembling at the urgency in their voices, I turned the radio on.

"Just do it!" Saharah demanded.

"I am, bitch! I am!" I yelled back. Turning the knob, flicking through the stations, I was finally there. I heard a female's voice speaking calmly to the station's audience. I listened intently.

"That bitch ain't dead. That's all I got to say." She hung up. I'd caught the ass-end of whatever my friends were so excited about. DJ Homer Blow was still trying to reach her.

"Caller, caller! Are you still there? I think we've lost her. Wow! The streets are talking. Sad, if true. I wouldn't hesitate to trade my life for any of my kids. I'm taking calls. Call in and let me know what you think. I wanna know how y'all feel about what you've just heard."

Putting the phone back to my ear, I turned the radio down. "Who was that? What was she talking about?" I asked.

Oletta said, "Girl, whoever that was say—"

"O, wait!" Saharah cut her off. "Zoi, we comin' over there. Give us ten minutes, okay? Your line is about to be blowing up. Don't answer the phone."

"Saharah, you know I gotta answer this phone! Why wouldju—"

"Damn, I forgot," she dryly replied.

"Somebody clicking in now. I'll see y'all in a minute."

"A'ight," she replied, before yelling: "Timber, hang up, I'm on my way to get y'all."

When I clicked over, it was my momma. She beat around the bush instead of just telling me. She'd asked a million questions before finally relaying to me what she'd just heard on the radio. My heart shattered. I couldn't believe my ears! Now I knew for sure that I wasn't going crazy, and me seeing Action wasn't just a figment of my imagination. *Oh my God! He's alive!* I thought to myself. But, the thin line between love and hate was immediately defined by her very next sentence.

Bang-bang-bang-bang-bang! Startled, I jumped. Somebody was banging on the front door. I'd dropped the phone. I could still hear my mother screaming my name through the receiver as my fretting soul caused me to fall to the floor. The tide of this world had my spirit twisted inside.

"It can't be! It can't beeee! No-no-no-nooooo!" I screamed, balled up in the fetal position. Tears blinded me as I tried to rid my mind of this being painfully true. My body shuttered. "Actiooooon! You muthafuckaaah! No-o-o-o-o!" *Bang-bang-bang-bang-bang!*

"Zoi, open this door!" Saharah yelled, but I couldn't move. I then heard four loud thuds before my door came crashing in, sending chills down my spine. Saharah had kicked it in. I lifted my head just enough to see their blurred silhouettes standing around me staring, as I curled up on my living room floor. I was devastated.

"They gon' kill my-my ba-byyyy!" I cried.

"Don't say that!" Saharah frowned.

"Zo, come on, girl! Get up!" Oletta knelt down and tugged at me.

"No-o-o-o-o! Ju-just leave me alonnne!" I yelled in a state of aggravated confusion. I snatched my shirt from her grasp.

"While y'all just standing there lookin' crazy! Help me get her up!" she yelled at Timber and Saharah. They'd scraped me off the floor. Pulling my limp body into their arms, they'd managed to fling me onto the couch.

"It's gon' be alright, Zee," Timber said, as she wiped my tears.

"Hello?" Oletta picked the phone up off the floor. "Oh, Ma? Girl, yo momma been on the phone all this time! We got her Ma." Saharah rubbed my back as I tried to pull it together.

Hanging the phone up, Oletta said, "Yo' momma nem on their way." I'd never felt so low. I felt like nothing but my baby could soothe my pain. Slightly above a whisper, I constantly asked myself, how could this be? How could he still be alive? How could he still be alive and not do any and everything to save our baby? In my mental emotional breakdown, I'd somehow fallen asleep. My dream took me back to the morning I'd found him.

***

The phone rang, bringing me out of my sleep. But, I'd paid it no mind at first. When I felt movement, and turned over to see he'd actually gotten up, and was standing next to the bed trying to quietly put on his jeans, my mind questioned what he was up to.

"Baby, where you going this early?" I asked with a yawn.

"I gotta handle somethin' real quick. Something happened to Rock, and I need to go see what up with him. Go back to sleep. I'll be back with some breakfast." He'd slapped me on my butt, which usually meant he'd be back for some morning sex alongside breakfast, so I smiled.

"Okay, babe. I'll see you when you get back." I rolled back over and closed my eyes. I'd heard him go in the master bathroom. The toilet flushed, then I heard the water running. As I dozed back off, my heart was hoping his ass wasn't cheating again. I was later awakened by a strange noise, causing me to sit up. I gazed at the clock that sat on the nightstand next to the bed. It read 6:02 AM. I shrugged it off, being I heard nothing else but silence. The baby was still

asleep, so patting my pillow, I laid back down. Then POOP! There it was again. What the hell? I thought to myself as sat back up. Let me go down here and see what this boy up to. I got up, wrapped myself in my Terry cloth robe, and slid into my slippers. I was still sluggish. Lolling through the hallway, I'd finally hit the stairs.

"Eric, you still here?" I called out, as I made it down the first set of steps and turned the corner leading to the next flight. "Action!" I yelled again, grabbing the baluster as I wearily climbed down the staircase. I got no answer. When I got to the bottom of the stairs, and looked to my left towards the living room; there he lay. He was sprawled out on the floor with one of my big throw pillows covering his head. Blood was everywhere. I ran over to him. Pulling the pillow from his face, I gasped. Seeing all that blood, and a bullet wound in his face, I panicked.

"Ahhhhhhhhhh! Ericccc! Help! Somebody help meeee!" I screamed, tears flushing from my eyes. He wasn't moving. My screams must have waken EJ, because I heard him crying. My gaze shifted, checking my surroundings. I had no idea if the person, or persons responsible were still in the house or not. I ran back upstairs and got my baby. Creeping back down the stairs, cradling him in my arms, I ran straight out the front door and over to the neighbor's house. I called his mother, like he'd always told me. She'd called the police. His mom got there within minutes of the police arriving in these dark Sedans. Minutes later, an ambulance and a few black and whites showed up. They'd taped the block off, and the yard as well. I was in shock! I couldn't find it in myself to go back in the house. All I could do was wait in wonder. Was he okay? I was leaning up against the neighbor's porch rail, smoking a cigarette when they brought his body out.

They had his head covered.

"Eriiiic! Eric!" I tried running to him, but I was stopped cold in my tracks by one of the officers securing the scene.

"Ma'am, I'm going to need you to step back for me!" he said.

"Bu-but that's my husband! This is my house!" I pointed desperately.

"I'm aware of that. I know he was your husband, ma'am. I'm sorry."

"Whatchu mean was! Is he—" I covered my mouth with both hands.

"Yes, I'm sorry to be the one to inform you. He's deceased. I lost it! "What! Move! N'aw, move! He-he ain't! Eric! Errriiic!"

As the officer held me, through bleary tears, I saw my mother-in-law getting into the ambulance with him.

"Wait! Mrs.Charlse! I wanna—I wanna gooo!" I tried to maneuver out of his grasp, but he held me tightly.

"Get-getcho hands off-a-me!" I screamed, as I struggled.

He said, "Stay calm. Just relax. I know you want to be with him. Unfortunately, you'll have to remain here for a while longer. We're going to have to ask you a few questions."

Chapter 17

The Lick
-Lue

98.7 and WNOV were both covering the highly publicized disappearance. I'd made an anonymous call while they were live on the air. I announced that the streets were talking. And they'd said not only was Eric Charlse Senior alive and well, but he'd also ordered the death of his own seed when offered a chance to exchange his son's life for his own. I'd figured I'd even the odds a little bit, instead of everybody simply looking for perpetrators behind the shit. I wonder if his ass was listening. If he wasn't, he'd find out soon enough. I set the city on fire with that shit! I'd done it without thinking though. I'd forgotten that Action knew we were responsible for taking Eric. He could've easily retaliated by putting us on blast in the same fashion. *Hood copped a crib for herself on North 20th. She was still in a predominantly black neighborhood. The only difference was that all the residents around her were old. Hell, you rarely saw any of them unless they were outside in the summer working in their gardens. But it was now winter and cold as a bitch! They were nowhere in sight. We officially had a new hangout. Hood's shit was dope. She had wall-to-wall white carpet which made your feet feel as though you were walking on cotton. There was the Italian furniture in cream leather to match. Her entertainment center and the 4,500-gallon fish tank were my favorites. The fish tank contained aquarium rock-sand, a "Do not enter" sign, a shit eater and her two sharks.*

She took it back to Africa with her decorating scheme. She had everything, from tribal masks, pictures, African vases and wicker, to really emphasize what she was trying to do. There were plants everywhere. Shit, he had us all ready to do the damn thang. But, as she explained, we had to stay "incognito."

Although her crib was for all of us, I can't front. I was jealous. We were all sitting in her living room on the soft leather, smoking good-good and sipping my favorite wine. Can you say Moscato? We had a few joints in rotation and I was high as shit! As we waited for the details on this next lick, we were taking votes. Everybody was on deck except Cyn, and I didn't like it one bit.

"Lue! Lue! You know you hear me, bitch! Damn, is you even here? Snap out off it!" Mula said, snapping her fingers. "You just gon' hold the bottle? I said I'm empty. Hit me up!"

"Oh! My bad, girl. This song had my ass somewhere else. The song—Let's Chill—by Guy was playing softly in the background. I leaned forward to fill her glass, but Hood put her hand over the top of it.

"Uh-un, Lue!" she said, "Hold up before you pour her ass another one. Mu, what's your decision on count of Sherrice? Is Cyn in, or is she out?"

"She's out! Now pour up!" Mula said.

"A'ight, I guess that settles it. She's out on this one," Hood replied.

"Hmmph!" I huffed and crossed my arms.

"A'ight, y'all, this what we gon' do," Hood said, looking around the room at us.

"Damn, bitch, pass the weed! You hoggin' the shit!" Sweets said, reaching for the joint. Hood smacked her fingers. We all laughed.

"Nah, here, my bad." Then she finally passed the J.

"I still don't see why Cyn ain't comin'," I said, "You hoes—"

"You hoes what?" Hood griped. "We already voted on the shit. Y'all lost three-ta-two! Damn, stop carryin' that shit. She out! End of discussion. Now listen. Lue, you listening?"

"Yeah, sis, I'm listening."

"A'ight." Hood continued. "Even though Atkinson Gold went missin', his man and 'nem ain't missed a beat. Them niggaz still over there catchin' good paper and we going to get it."

"Bri, you used to fuck wit' Ready," Mula said. "You sure you good on this?"

"Bitch, please don't ever question my P.Y.T. Let's go get this money." Bri blew out her smoke and said, "Sweets used to fuck wit' T-Dog. I'ont see nobody questionin' her."

"Well, excuse me, bitch. Damn, I wasn't questioning your touch, I was just askin'," Mu said, rollin' her eyes.

"Me and that nigga been through when I caught him with that hoe, Tameera, off 31st," Bri said.

"So, you'll pop'em?" Sweets asked.

"Wit' no hesitation and no regret. Damn, you questioning me too?"

"Nah, we just gotta know. I mean, him being yo' first and all."

"Shit, you think? That gives me all the more reason. The nigga burnt me, remember?"

"Hell yeah, I remember!" Hood replied. "You was talkin' about killin' his ass back then. Was you serious?"

"I dunno, I was only thirteen. But I'm serious now. Can we get back to the money please! Y'all trippin'! If it comes to it I'll kill'em, a'ight? Now next. What we gon' do?"

"Daaammnn, you were thirteen?" I said. I hadn't heard that story.

"Not now, Lue." Bri said, waving me off.

I sucked my teeth. "Later then, bitch," I said, "Don't be mad at me. I ain't the one that burntchu." I smiled, and she rolled her eyes.

"It's a short notice, but bro 'nem put me up on these niggaz last night," Hood said, "Bri, you down to play with Ready for a few days?"

"Damn, me again! I knew this shit was comin' when you mentioned dem niggaz." Bri looked bitter, taking a sip of her drink.

"Shit, I need a personal joint now. Shit!"

"Bri, don't even trip, boo-boo. If you goin' in, I'm witchu." Sweets hit the weed. "I owe you that much. I'm the reason you met the nigga so—" she blew out her smoke. "I got T-Dog. He's been dyin' to get some more of dis pussy."

"Whatchu say, Bri?" Hood asked.

"I'm in," Bri replied.

"Y'all know bro 'nem used to get money wit them niggaz, right?" Hood asked.

Mula said, "Yeah, we know. Annnd?" She took a sip of her drink.

"It's sweet, I'm tellin' you! We—"

"Wait! Wait-wait-wait! Excuse me," I protested, "But didn't yo' ass just get grazed in the neck like—" I frowned, taking a toke. "I think we should be cool for a minute. Just being honest."

"Lue, it's just a scratch. That nigga ain't did shit!" Now she too was waving me off.

She said, "Yo' lil' ass need to be cool," she pointed. "Don't call nobody else. We gettin' this money." I was through trying to argue.

"Well, whatchu want us to do?" Bri questioned.

"I don't know. Do something nice. We just need y'all to screen the niggaz for a few days to make sure we don't miss nothin'."

Sweets said, "That's cool. I got an idea."

Looking at her sideways, Bri said, "Uh-oh! Whatchu thinkin', bitch? I know your ideas."

Moistening her lips, Sweets said, "Bri, chill-lax. You'll like it, damn! You know I luh you." She smiled. Four of us laughed, but Bri ain't see a damn thang funny.

It was on, but Teague and the twins didn't want us involved, period. We hadn't done our jobs. Hood couldn't relax though. It ain't in her. She was still brainstorming and plotting our next move. Bri and Sweets were the lucky ones. They got to go to the Bahamas!

I couldn't believe they'd treated T-Dog and Ready super 'ugly' asses to an exotic island like that! But, if it was gon' lead us to some easy money, I guess. Hood got tired of the rest of us poutin' and we'd flown out to Vegas. Me and Cyn were only able to stay over the weekend though. We were still in school. Plus, she had to get back to her baby. I just couldn't wait until everybody got back. We ain't know what happened to the baby, and we were forbidden from asking any questions. The shit was nerve-wrecking. Niggaz dyin' left and right! On top of that, Mula and Hood crazy asses were calling every other day, talking about sending them more and more money. They'd been there for weeks, and had blown through thirty-thousand dollars! It was time for them to bring their asses home! Fuck that shit!

Chapter 18

Cyn

We were back home and at a standstill while everybody else was still out of town. In my divided mind, self control was something I didn't have at the time. Lue didn't make it any better. She was on my ass. I didn't know if I should get out and ring the buzzer, pull up and blow my horn, or go to a payphone and try to call him again. It had been weeks, and I still hadn't heard from him. He wasn't answering his phone, so I struck a deal with Lue.

She agreed to ride to Racine with me, if I'd roll out to the prison with her to see Honor. We'd been out there in the midst of snow flurries for about 15 to 20 minutes. She'd grown tired of my bullshit.

"Pull up, bitch! Why you park all the way down here! I know we ain't came all this way to burn gas and let the heat blow! Shit, I mean, really? We just gon' look at the condo? You want me to ring that mug? I'll do it if you scared." She bounced around in the passenger seat of the Mercedes, giving me that colorful bubbly personality of hers.

She said, "You know he in there! There goes his car right there. Whatchu gon' do?" She folded her arms across her chest, looking me upside my head.

"I don't know! I jus—"

"Cynnn! Uh-uhn! Look!" she pointed. There she was, coming out the foyer doors wrapped in a chinchilla with the matching hat.

She was lookin' cute in her black jeans and grey boots.

"Mmmmm! Look-a-here! Look-a-here! That's why you ain't heard from his black ass!" Lue curled her lips to the side. Seeing her made me mad, but seeing he soon followed had my blood boiling. I started to get out and act a donkey on his ass and this chica. But Lue grabbed my arm as they got in the car.

"N'aw, let's follow'em and see where they goin'," she suggested.

I should've just taken my ass to the crib.

But, being curious and stupid, I listened.

We were in traffic, *boom*. Tell me why we ended up out at Regency Mall, following them though the tapestry of shoppers. Chick-Fil-A had the south entrance of the mall smelling good as we walked in. It was about 3:30 in the evening and the mall was super busy due to the holidays. Blending in wasn't a problem at all. The laughter, chatter and smiles from patrons, food vendors and department store employees said, '*Tis the season*. Christmas jingles were in the air at every turn. The aroma of pizza lured noses in one direction, while the scent of freshly baked Cinn-A-Buns and chocolate chip cookies tempted others. Everybody seemed as though they were filled with the Spirit, but me. Seeing this bitch was killing my vibe. Her name is Terry. She's the mother of his son. She's very pretty, and, like me, she has a sense of taste, and could dress her ass off. From Niemann's, Victoria's Secret, Boston Store, DJ's to Wilson's Leather, they browsed from store to store. She had Money carrying all types of bags. She reminded me of me.

You can imagine how I felt watching them turn heads as they strolled the promenade. Though jealousy and envy had me feeling overwhelmed, I was cool. I could handle it. So I thought. When they stopped at Kay's, I lost it. Lue had to hold me back. What the fuck they doin' at Kay's! I had to get up out that mall before I snapped! *Was he buying her a ring?* I thought to myself.

"Aw-hell-n'all!" I was on that! She grabbed me.

"Sis, pipe down. I see whatchu seeing, but chill. He might be just buying her a Pandora bracelet or somethin'."

"Let me go, Lue! I'm good." I nodded to myself as tears welled from my eyes. She turnt me loose and we walked off, heading out. Back at the Benz, I hit the alarm and we got in. Starting it up, I sat there for a minute with my eyes closed. For some reason I felt like I'd been running. I couldn't catch my breath.

"Man, Cyn. This was a bad idea. I'm sorry." Lue tried to console me.

"Don't be," I replied, putting the car in reverse. Looking over my shoulder, I backed outta the parking spot. When we exited the mall's huge parking lot, turning onto the main road, she just looked at me. She'd noticed we weren't heading towards I-94. We were actually heading back towards the inner city.

She said, "I know you ain't!"

"Nah, I'm not. We are." I turned to her with a cold stare. "Mayyyyybe, this wasn't such a bad idea after all. We goin' in."

"How you know ain't nobody else in there? You know he keep a gang of nigguhs wit'em." she questioned.

"I guess we're about to find out, huh?"

Alexander Grandbell was on Hot 102. I turned it up, and put the pedal to the floor singing. "Sunday, Monday, Tuesday, Wednesday, Thursday, Friday, Saturdayyy!"

The ten-minute ride took me all of five, running a few lights. Pulling back into the Bell Harbor skyscraper condominiums, Lue was having second thoughts.

She said, "I don't know, Cyn. I ain't feeling too good about this one."

"Shh! Just shut up and come the hell on! We've done worse. A lot worse." I shrugged.

I didn't even give her a chance to respond. I cut the engine off, jumped out, ran over to the entrance and rang the buzzer like I was losing my mind. It didn't take her long to catch up. The intercom was silent, which told me there was nobody else in the apartment.

"Bitch, it's broad daylight and we finna do this shit?" she whispered, huddling closely behind me with her hands in her coat pockets. The fur around the seams of her purple Bomber's hood concealed her face. Being reckless, I really didn't give a fuck who saw me.

"Lue, when I said we were goin' in, you didn't think I meant breaking in, did you? I got the keys. I just gotta figure out which ones they are." The lobby key always looks different from the rest, so that was obvious. I picked the odd one. I slid the teeth in the lock of the glass door's entrance to the hallway, and guess what? It turned. I'd made copies of every key on his keyring when we were planning to hit'em. Nervously, I watched the floor counter on the elevator we'd boarded. I was hoping he hadn't changed the locks upstairs. We hit the 5th floor. He stayed in unit 531. Hurrying down the hallway, we were finally at the door. I stuck the first key in the door, but it wouldn't turn. The second concluded the same results. Lue was gettin' antsy.

"Come'onnn! Whatchu doin'? White people walkin' through this mutha-fucka, girl!" she hissed through her teeth.

"A'ight! I got two more to try, damn." Putting the third key in the lock, the teeth fit perfectly. It struck the tumbling pin, and with the turn of the key I unlocked the door. We went in. I closed the door behind us.

Lue said, "What if they come back?"

"Trust me, they ain't done spending money. He told me how she like to shop. They're just gettin' started." I smiled at her over my shoulder. "Now stop worrying. And, like Denzel said in *Glory,* tear it uuup! Tear this bitch up!"

Money was a creature of habit. Just like the crib he shared with me, this one was laced. The stained cherry-wood floors were nice and shiny throughout the living room and dining room. The walls were milk-white, and the ceilings were high. There was white leather and a huge Persian rug in the middle of the floor to match. Glass tables, brass animals and all the expensive decor were real nice. After kicking in his speakers, breaking all the TVs and cutting up his furniture, while Lue did damage to the dinning room, I went straight for the closets. I couldn't find any scissors, so I settled for a knife I'd gotten from the kitchen to stab his shit up. Em-hmm! I sure did! Terry was lucky she didn't have any personal belongings there. Me and Lue went through the entire apartment, tearing that muthafucka up like Tyler Perry and Kimberly Elise did in *Diary of a Mad Black Woman*. That's right! He'd brought the Madea outta bitch! Back in the car, we were breathless with excitement.

"Whew!" Lue said, breathing hard. "We didn't get a dime, but at least we got up out of there! You a'ight? You feel better?"

"A little." I looked at her and smiled. We'd pulled out the parking lot heading home, just as the Jakes were pulling in.

Chapter 19

Hood

We had a blast out in Vegas! But it felt good to be home. Bri and Sweets had a bunch of questions about our trip, just as we had inquiries concerning theirs. We were at All-Star's gettin' our bowl on in the midst of noshing on some chicken tenders and some Chili-cheese fries. It was surprisingly packed to be a Thursday night. The continuous rumbling flow of bowling balls sliding down the heavily polished lanes striking the tenpins sounded like a thunder storm. The dimly lit, low-ceiling bunker like structure of the establishment was alive with people having a good time. We couldn't believe it, but it just so happened to be Cyn's first experience. We'd actually had to talk her into trying it. Being the fashion monger she is, she was reluctant to putting on the brown and off-white shoes. Indeed, they were some old, ancient and frightful looking things altogether. But, they'd have to do. Her gripe was that they didn't match her outfit. However, she had a change of heart once she realized that her ass wouldn't be able to play without them. We had a small wager on our hands. The team that lost had to cough up the bread for our next hair, nail and spa treatments. At one-eighty-nine, Mula holds the best bowling average of us all, so everybody wanted to be on her team. Her mother was a bowling champ and had taught her well. She and I were captains, and she'd decided she'd pick up Cyn and Sweets. It was me, Bri and Lue against them.

To me, we held the advantage. Because that meant Mu had to bowl, coach and teach. We were down to our last couple frames, and they had us ninety-one to eighty-three. But, we were in luck. Cyn was up again.

"I can't do it! My nails too long for this shit!" she cursed.

"You don't have to put your fingers in the holes, Cyn! It's all in the wrist. You got this!" Mula yelled, as she reclined in her seat. Wincing, the owner of the building watched intently as she lined up for her next shot. She'd thrown and dropped a few balls that could've done some serious damage to the lane. He was on the verge of puttin' all our asses out. As loud as we were, to those on the outside looking in, we may have appeared to be drunk. But none of us liked beer. We had to stay on point, so they kept that in the taps along with all that other shit they had behind the bar. As far as we were concerned, we were doing fine drinking Pop. Cyn had the ball hoisted in front of her face in her stance. Her lips were pursed in concentration, the tip of her tongue slightly sticking out the side.

Bri yelled, "I don't see it in you!"

"Me neither!" I co-signed. "Face it. You-just-can't-bowl." I shook my head as she glanced back at us.

Lue said, "You's a guttah bitch! Come' on! Wooo! Wooo-oooh! Give us one more in the gutter!" she clapped. "Y'all don't need them points!"

"Guttah biiitch, guttah-bitch, gutter-bitch!" we sang in unison in an attempt to throw her off.

Though she'd bowled more gutter balls than anything, she'd also managed to produce a spare outta that mess. We needed this game. Mula's team always won, since she was known for strikes. At times, I hated auntie had won all those damn trophies. If Cyn fucked this up, we might stand a chance.

Guttah-biiitch, gutta-bitch, gutter-bitch!" me and mine continued to sing our song.

Feeling impelled to comfort her, Sweets screamed, "Don't listen to'em, Cyn! You got this!"

I yelled, "Not to-dayyy! Not to-niiight! Guttah-biiitch!"

"The wrist! Flick the wrist!" Mula commanded.

"Cyn, is that the right ball?" Lue questioned.

"Yeah, I don't know." Bri laughed. "I think that one might be too heavy for you."

"Will y'all shut-the-hell-up! I got it!" she yelled back in frustration. She swung the ball back and let it go. Her release was smooth. The ball rode the right hand rail as she jumped up and down, praying that it didn't fall in the gutter. It looked as though it was about to do just that, when it suddenly hooked and veered left, crashing into the pins.

"Yeeeeeah! Ha-ha-haaaa!" Cyn laughed. She was fired up, pumpin' her little fist. She ran over to Sweets and Mu, giving out hugs and high fives as they stood to applaud her. She even had the nerve to stick her damn tongue out at us. Her happy-go-lucky ass rolled a strike in the 1-3 pocket. They were celebrating like it was over. I didn't wanna hear the song or see the dance. But, we were down, and they were trying to be funny.

"We gettin' pampered! We gettin' pammm-pered!" they sang, doing the Cabbage Patch on our ass. Lue was up, and we needed her to come through.

"That's a'ight! We good!" I yelled, trying to remain optimistic. "Bring it in!" I brought my team to a huddle. "We straight, " I whispered. "We just saved the best for last. Lue, hit'em with the Grand-mah-mah."

"The Grand-mah-mah!" Bri reiterated.

"Y'all sure?" she questioned, since it didn't always work.

"Hell yeah," I reassured her. "I don't know why I didn't think of it earlier."

She said, "Okay, one grandma coming right up."

Coming outta the huddle, I gave Mu and her team a calm resolute stare.

"Uh-ohh! It's Lue's turn!' I cheered, clapping my hands.

"Get'em, Lue!" Bri shouted, as she grabbed her favorite ball and lined up for her shot. They had no idea what we were up to, until Lue squatted down and swung the ball between her legs using both hands. The bowling ball slowly glid down the lane as we laughed hysterically. I don't know how, but Lue had somehow managed to master the art of bowling like an old lady. It usually resulted in a strike. Knocking down eight of ten pins, she'd left the seven and the ten standing. Mula was up next. She struck our asses again! It was over with. You should've seen'em. Hoopin' and hollerin' like they'd just won a million bucks. Lue wore a hangdog expression on her face as she flopped down in her seat.

She dropped her head into her forearms as they rested on the table.

"Okay! Okayyy already. Calm down, y'all won." I sat down next to Lue and rubbed her back. "It's gon' be a'ight. We'll get'em next time. Raising her head, she cracked a smile.

She said, "Psyyych! I ain't mad." She laughed. "Just puttin' on a show for our opponents and them dudes a few lanes down. They keep staring every chance they get. As Lue waved, we glanced their direction. The dudes averted their eyes, but their female companions continued to stare.

"Aw, them fools!" I threw my hands up. All we saw were noses flaring, lips smackin' and necks roll as they expressed whatever it was they had on their minds to the dudes they were with. I said, "Fuck'em, let'em look. They ain't on shit." I rolled my eyes and my neck right back. "Anyways!" I yelled, flipping them off. Turning my attention back to the squad, I said, "Fill us in on y'all trip. What happened?"

"Yeah, y'all, how was it?" Mula questioned.

Sweets said, "Oh, it was beautiful! We gotta go back."

"Ooh! Sounds like home." Cyn smiled, taking a sip of her Tahiti Treat.

Bri said, Sure was! We was out there in our lil' two pieces and errythannng! Bikinied uuuup!" she blushed.

"And you know iiiiit! Wait a minute!" Sweets echoed, waving her arm and snapping her fingers.

"The parties over there don't stop! And the nigguhz!" Bri pounded the table. I had to stop her ass right there.

"Hold up! Whatchu do? I know y'all didn't?"

Bri said, "Nah, Hood. We stuck to the script. I mean, she handled her end a little different or better than I did but we played nice. Huh, Sweets? Didn't I?" Bri looked for confirmation.

"She let him have a lil' fun. He got a couple kisses and some touches here and there. But, that's 'bout it!" We laughed. "Nigga probably got blue-balls as we speak." Sweets dropped her gaze. "I gotta keep it real though. Somewhere in the mix, the old feelings I had for T-Dog came flooding back."

"Awww, shit." I huffed.

"I ended up giving him a quickie."

"Ooooh! Look atchu, whorin'! You nasty!" I pointed, giving her a stern look as we all gasped.

She said, "What? Don't be lookin' at me all bugeyed! I—I was horny, I just took him for a dance. Y'all wanted in, right?" She folded her arms across her chest. "We in." Studying her face, I broke into a warm smile.

"Everything good?" I asked.

"We good. Trust!" Sweets nodded.

Bri said, "Now tell us about Vegas!"

"Yeah, go 'head and tell'em! Tell'em how yo' ass almost left us high and dry in the desert." Mula crossed her legs.

"Shut up, Mu! We came out a'ight. We had a ball out there! Let me tell y'all."

Chapter 20

Vegas
Hood

As we descended, it didn't look like much but miles on top of miles of barren desert. Then, we passed a big lake and a humongous dam, smack dead in the middle of all that sand. All of sudden, there it was on the horizon. Vegas! We'd landed, and I couldn't believe it. The city that matched the stars with all its lights. It was like I'd fallen asleep and woke up in Oz. There was so much to see as we rode through the city, heading towards the huge sand-colored pyramid that's said to be the strongest beam of light on earth at its peak. That's right, we were staying at the Luxor! Out front stands this huge replica of the Sphinx. You know, the mythical Egyptian monster with the human head and the body of a lion? When I'd asked the receptionist at the front desk what the Sphinx symbolized, she'd told us it represented the Pharaoh as an incarnation of the sun god, Ra. The Luxor has 2,521 rooms in that bitch, and were staying in two suites on the 3rd floor from the top! We were actually transported to our rooms in something that felt like a magical spaceship of some sort. It's hard to explain without you being there. But the hotel has these inclined elevators that move on an angle up the side of the the pyramid. Teague told me the Lux was nice, but I had no idea it was like that! That shit was dope! Anyway, we were all hungry after the flight. So, we unpacked, showered up, changed and went in search of some food inside the hotel.

Everything sounded good. Since we were four deep and we all had taste for something different, we decided we'd hit all seven eateries the hotel had to offer before heading home. That first night, we treated ourselves and dined in their gourmet room called *Isis*. We'd entered through this long colonnade walkway past what appeared to be ancient caryatid statues. There were these huge glass doors with embossed wings. The mezzanine level overlooking the casino had us feeling like Egyptian queens as we quietly laughed and made small talk over dinner. We'd eaten and finished off a two-thousand dollar bottle of Lafite Rothschild. Shit, the wine had us turnt all the way up! Whachu say? Lit? So, it was time to hit the streets.

I said, "Y'all know what time it izzzz! We're herrrre!" I raised my glass.

"Ahhhhhhhhhh!" we screamed in unison.

45 Minutes Later...

I was to blind to see / When you belonged to me / You were my everything / Now I'd give anything / To feel the love you bring / You were my eveything—

Cyn was drivin'. I was in the passenger seat. Lue and Mula were in the back. We were bobbing our heads and snappin' our fingers as we cruised up the strip, singing along to Jody Watley's hit, *Everything*.

We'd pulled to the stoplight at the intersection of Flamingo and Las Vegas Boulevard when Lue started feelin' herself a lil' too much. How could I blame her? As beautiful as we are, you know we were catching the same ole vibes from the haters. Hoes turning up their noses and shit. It ain't our fault if their dudes wanna holla.

She yelled, "Yea-eeeahh! Ha-haaa! Whaasup, bitcheeesss!" towards the crowd as she stood in the backseat of the droptop black Benz we'd rented. Smiling, I'd glanced back to make sure her crazy ass didn't still have her heels on. We couldn't be tearing shit up that we had to take back.

"Girl, sitcho butt down. You gon' get us pulled over," I told her as we grooved to the music.

She said, "Dayum! Who is that pullin' up behind us in the Rolls!"

"Where?" Cyn said, turning the volume down. We all looked back.

Mula said, "Whoever it is, is being chauffeured. And it looks like they got a car full of women." We were breaking our necks trying to see who in the money-green foreign Corniche thang! The car pulled alongside of us, and we heard music as the back window slowly came down. The music ceased, and we heard laughs and giggles from the females' inside. It was dark, and whoever it was, he was a chocolate something. We couldn't make out who he was. He had a distinctive voice that I thought was familiar as he spoke. We heard him say, "Yo, chill for a second. St-stop suckin' it. Okay, ooh! Just a little bit though. Ladi—ladies! Yo, y'all should come to *The Landmark* tonight around 2:30! It's across the street from the Hilton!"

"Who is that!" Mula yelled, hanging out the drop in an attempt to get a better view. Those behind us at the light grew impatient and began blowing their horns. The light was green, and we'd held up traffic.

He said, "Zip, turn the light on real quick so they can see a nigga." The interior lights came on, and we lost our minds.

"Ahhhhhh!" I screamed in excitement. "Tha—that's!"

Flashing a smile, he said, "It's Brooklyn Baby!" and the Rolls Royce sped off.

"That was Tyson! That was Iron Mike mutha-fuckin' Tysonnn!" Cyn screeched as she turned the corner.

I said, "Yup! The nigga was getting his dick sucked, and still stopped to holla at us! Heeey! Now that's boss shit! Geh me some!" I threw my fist up. Lue and Cyn gave me some dap, but Mu left me hangin'. She was disgusted.

She said, "Uh-unn! Them bitches is nasty!" She had her face all curled up.

After we'd rode for a while, we decided to get out and walk. We had tickets to see the light show with the fountains outside *The Bellagio*. Dudes were coming at us from all directions. We gave up some conversation, got a few numbers and kept it movin'. We couldn't and wouldn't dare pass on the invitation Iron had extended. It was a must that we hit *The Landmark*. We noticed a fleet of luxury vehicles upon our arrival. Although we shouldn't have been surprised, we were wowed to see Eddie Murphy pull in the parking lot. He jumped out of a black-on-black Lamborghini Diablo. We just had to get that autograph. Security was trippin'! They didn't wanna let us in at first, claiming Cyn and Lue looked too young. I made their ass go get Mike. He straightened that shit out with the quickness, and we were granted access.

Upon entry, we were each handed a bottle of Dom Perignon. To match his attire, the nigga— Tyson—had the entire club laced in Versace! From the wallpaper, cups, table cloths all the way down to the napkins. He wasn't playin'. Mind you, this is before the urban communities had the slightest idea who the legendary designer was. We recognized that a number of celebrities had come out to join Mike and enjoy the Vegas nightlife. Naomi Campbell was in the building, and looking stunning as ever. However, seeing her brought back memories of Egypt and her crew. My thoughts had me in my chest for a minute. There were a few pounds set out in the V.I.P. section, so I grabbed us some weed. I asked the squad to step outside with me to put a few in the air for momma and Shebba. We didn't shed any tears that night. Instead we shared smiles, as we blew the 'Ooh-wee' and sent a few words up to'em. Sparking a flame, I looked at the sky.

"I know y'all lookin' down. Just know that I miss you."

"We miss y'all too! She ain't the only one!" Mula interjected. Lue just closed her eyes and dropped her head. Cyn popped the cork on her bottle and spilled some on the concrete.

She said, " I've heard so much about y'all." She took a swig and handed me the bottle. She said, "Shebba, that son of yours is something else!"

Lue said, "We know you see'em. Girrrrl, he's bad as hell! Im'a whup his lil' behind!" she nodded.

"No, you ain't." I smiled. "You ain't gon' hit nothin' but this drink and this reefa. Here." I passed her the Dom.

"Yes, I am. Watch," she replied softly. I hit the weed.

"Ma, Sis! Can y'all believe we're at this party in Las Vegas and it's multi-million dollar niggaz in the building! Nah, I know. Chill. Shebba, tell Ma, we chillin'. We ain't on that tonight. I promise!" I said, gruffly blowing out the smoke.

Mula said, "Sure-in-the-hell ain't! We ain't fuckin' with Mike Tyson crazy ass! The bitch Robin Givens said he'd knocked her the fuck out!"

"He ain't hit that damn lady. If he had, her head would've looked like six footballs instead of one. His ass would've been in jail!" Cyn replied, taking a sip of her champagne.

"He did!" Mula protested." *Aw shit—Here we go*, I thought to myself. They got to debating.

Anyway, we couldn't have made a move even if we wanted to. We'd left the guns at the crib. We were there to have fun, so we got lifted. We rejoined the party and got lifted some more. We ended up dancing, smokin' weed and sippin' Dom until the sun rose. I was fucked up! Somehow, when I woke up, we were back at the Luxor. All I remember is opening my eyes and yelling, "I'm hungry!" Excitedly, it was time to do it all over again.

Chapter 21

Hood
-Sharnetta

Lue and Cyn were flying back in the morning, so we had to go ham! Meaning, hard as a muthafucka! So, that's what we did. We balled out! Shopping, eating, spa treatment, the works. I can't personally speak for everybody else, but there's one particular someone that made Vegas a place I'll remember for a lifetime. We were standing at the blackjack table in the MGM Grand when I noticed her and her friends walking through the casino. I couldn't help but notice how her friends followed her every move. Her energy was magnifying. Her presence was simply captivating. It's what I call *powerful*. She wore her hair in these saucy spirals. She was a redbone, standing about 5'7", and thick in all the right places. I could tell she had a few years on me. She was wearing this all-black Halston Heritage dress, with a black Dennis Basso fur. Frankly, I couldn't take my eyes off her. They were playing Poker, and from the looks of things, they must have been pretty good at it. They'd been at the same table for hours.

"Hood, you a'ight? We lost again, bitch! What we gon' do?" Mula asked, bringing me out of my daze. By this time, Cyn and Lue had been home for at least two weeks. Me and Mula were still trying to get it!

I said, "Fuck this game. Let's go over to the Poker table."

"But, you said—"

"I know. Just come on. I think I spotted somethin'!"

"Ooh! Is it a lick?" she asked, rubbing her hands together.

"I don't know. Just follow me."

We were walking in the direction in which the ladies were seated, when Mula stopped me, grabbing me by my arm.

"Uh-un, Hood! That's the tournament table! We ain't got no more chips."

"Well, we'll buy some! Hell, we ain't broke." I smiled mischievously.

"Not yet." She sighed, rolling her eyes.

We sat down at the table across from the crew and the men that had gathered to admire their beauty. Why not give their thirsty asses something more to drool over! We were dressed to kill, as always.

"The buy-in is 10k, ladies!" the dealer announced. She looked up at us, but I couldn't see her eyes, since they were hidden behind shades.

I said, "Mula, grab forty real quick."

"Forty what?" she replied. She had her mouth hung open, lookin' at me like I belonged in a straightjacket.

"Forty-thousand worth of chips!" I nudged her, talking through my teeth.

"Hood, you buggin'! All we got left is—"

"Girl, get the damn chips," I leaned in and whispered. She reluctantly searched in her purse and grabbed our last, pouting as she slammed each of the ten-thousand dollar stacks on the table. We heard chortling coming from the ladies across the table. Then, full blown laughter from all of them.

"Damn, she looks maaaad!" the leader of the crew scoffed, shaking her head. Her girls giggled. I ain't see a damn thing funny. You know I had to shoot back though. My bitch was pissed at me.

"And you look good enough to eat right now." I licked my lips and smiled.

"No, she didn't!" Her chocolate friend with the grey eyes rolled her neck and stood up. Their leader grabbed her arm, pulling her back into her seat.

I politely told her, "You can getchu a piece." I ain't know who she thought she was. Or who I was neither.

"Chill, Steph. I got this. Excuse me, sweetheart. First of all, what exactly do you mean?" she questioned.

I said, "You know exactly what I mean. What that pussy like?" I winked.

"Oooh! Ha-haaa! She's a bold one!" she clapped, looking at her crew. Tilting her head to the side, she folded her hands gracefully. She was staring at me as if she was trying to look through me. She said, "I'm flattered, but you are very disrespectful, love. Where you from?" She took her shades off, showing me her big beautiful brown eyes.

"Why? Where y'all from?" I asked.

One of her home girls, giving me sass, said, "Dade County, baby! M-I-A! Just-like-dat-dere!"

I said, "We from Milwaukee County. Y'all know where dat at?"

"Dang, they got black folk up dem-ways?" another asked. They all laughed. I rolled my eyes.

"Tuh!" Mu hissed at the crew.

Turning my attention back towards the head bitch in charge, I said: "But, anyways—"

She said, "In reference to your question, this pussy like Heaven. Errybody ain't goin'. Now, you sure y'all don't wanna keep y'all l'il money?" Once again, her girls were cracklin'.

"Our money good. There's a lot more where this came from," Mula assured them.

Her caramel friend said, "Don't tell'em nuttin' Netta! We can split that!"

I looked at the dealer and said, "Gon' deal! What we waitin' on? You being nosey?"

"Suit yourself." Netta shrugged.

They were all in possession of 50,000 or more in chips. Our stacks were extremely low in comparison. I refused to be bullied. But, boy did they try! I had to put my Poker face on, holdin' some and foldin' others. Mu ain't know what the hell she was doing. She was broke within a few hours. I'd put her back in several times before she'd decided that she'd had enough. The rest of us played and talked shit throughout the night, and well into the morning.

In the end, we had ourselves a standoff. Just me and her. Though most of her crew had retired to their suites, she had one faithful soldier that remained by her side. We were drunk, and could barely keep our eyes open. Mula ass was sleep and didn't even know it. Every time I said her name, she'd holla, "Huh? I ain't sleep", never opening her eyes, as her body swayed from side to side. This bitch wouldn't budge, and neither would I. I was up five times what I'd sat down with, but she still had me covered. I was dealt a pair of Aces. The game was Texas Holding.

"Sharnetta, look I'm tired! It's nine-o'clock in the fuckin' mornin'. Will you bitches just call it even and cash-da-hell-out! I'm falling asleep!" JoVonna yawned and stretched, resting her head on Sharnetta's shoulder.

"Fuck it, I'm all in!" Sharnetta exclaimed with confidence.

In my head, I'm thinking: *Okay, I got twins. Ain't nothing out there on the flop but a two of Hearts, a Jack of Spades, and a six of Diamonds. But wait! N'aw, she got a Jack. But, what if she got two Jacks?* I exhaled as I contemplated my next move. I said, *fuck it* as well and just asked her:

"Whatchu got? A Jack?" She just looked at me. "I think you bluffin', bitch. I call."

The dealer flipped the turn and the river. A six of Hearts, and queen of Clubs. *Fuck!* I said to myself.

He said, "Okay, ladies! Dress up time! What do you have?"

She flipped her cards. She was holding two Jacks all along. She had a mutha-fuckin' boat! I sucked my teeth, throwing the cards across the table. I grabbed Mula as the dealer announced what I'd already known.

"Full House! Mrs. Sharnetta wins!"

"Mula!" I yelled.

"Huh? I ain't sleep!" she swayed. I tugged her arm, and she damn near fell off the stool.

"You is sleep! Getcho ass up! Let's go!" I griped.

Sharnetta said, "Aw, Hood! Where y'all goin'?" I ignored her ass.

"Damn, what happened?" Mula questioned as I walked ahead. I was mad as hell!

"You lost, didn'tchu?" she asked. I thought it was obvious.

I said, "Just come on! We out. She wiped me down. We broke."

"N-o-o-o! Hood! All of it? You lost everything? How the fuck are we supposed to eat, get gas or do anything? We gon' have to call—"

"It's gon' be a'ight! Damn, you giving me a headache! Just let me think. Once we get back to the hotel I'll figure something out."

We'd walked. The Lux was only a few blocks away. I saw Mula safely to the suite, but I couldn't think sittin' still.

I headed back out. I told Lue and Cyn not to send us another dime. No matter what. I may have to eat those words.

Chapter 22

Bag of Money

Faded after taking a few joints to the face, I'd been walking the the strip for about an hour when a white stretch drove down on me. Sharnetta popped up out the sunroof like a jack-in-the-box, dabbing her face with some of the stacks she'd rightfully taken from me.

"She said, "Just the one I've been looking for! Hood, what up? Whew! This money smells good! Can you smell it?" Lowering the money, she smiled.

"Fuck you, Sharnetta. You won, now gon'!" I kept it movin' as the car eased along beside me.

"Bitch, you mad? You talked all that shit to me all night. You mad? By the way, you know I ain't mad." I guess she didn't get it verbally, so I gave her the finger.

She said, "Nah, I'm just playin'. Fa-real though, get in. I wanna holla atchu." I stopped and looked at her.

She said, "On some real shit. Just me and you. Woman to woman. All bullshit to the side." Begrudgingly, I got in and closed the door. Whitney Houston's *You Give Good Love* was playing softly in the background, though no speakers were visible.

"Just drive for now," she instructed her chauffeur. As I looked around, the inside of the limousine was immaculate.

I said, "Damn, you rented this?" *I need to ride in one of these more often*, I thought too myself.

She said, "Nope, this me. This is how I roll."

She reached over and grabbed a white bag with *Giorgio Armani* scrolled across both sides. "I'm glad you saw things my way and got in. Here you go, girl. This is for you." She handed me the bag. Opening it, I looked inside. I thought, *What tha—!*

Lookin' at her in disbelief, I asked: "What's this?"

"That's ninety-thousand right there. I put an extra fifty on top of the forty y'all lost as a gift." She crossed her legs and folded her hands.

"But—"

"No buts. That's you. Now, let's kick it. You hungry?" She looked me in my eyes.

"Yeah, I guess I could eat somethin'." I smiled, scooting a lil' closer to her.

"Wait a minute now! I know what you're thinking. I'm not talking about me, crazy! That's not what this is about, so stop!"

"Stop what?"

"Stop lookin' at me like that. I gotta a nigga at home, and he's as loyal as they come."

"Lookin' atchu like what?" I smiled.

"I'm talking food. You do know what that is, don't you?" she laughed, shaking her head.

"Of course I do. We can eat, but it's on me. It's the least I can do. I mean—" I nodded towards the bag of money.

"I wasn't on that! You trippin'." I laughed nervously.

"Emm-hm." She twisted her lips to the side. "Miguel, take us over to *The Rio*!" she yelled. "This place has the best breakfast in Vegas. You wanna stop and grab yo' girl—Mula?"

"Nah, she's knocked out. I'll grab her something to go. Hold up. I still don't understand though. We was gamblin'. Why would you give me all this money? What would make you do something like this?" I questioned.

"What made you come sit down? You don't think I saw you eyeing me all night? We're more alike than you know.

Besides, money comes and goes. It's not everything. It's paper. It don't mean shit. Some of us are simply blessed or cursed to have more than others. However, a friendship can last forever when it's genuine. And to be perfectly honest, I see something in you that I once saw in myself."

"Oh yeah? What's that?" I asked.

"Your pain. It's in your words. I see it in your eyes. I'd like to talk to you about it. That's if you don't mind?"

"Nah, I don't mind. Whatchu wanna know?"

"Let's start with your name. What did your mother chose for you? I know damn well it wasn't *Hood*."

"Ha-haaa!" I laughed. "No she didn't." I dropped my head. "It's Tasha," I replied, looking into her eyes.

"How old are you, Tasha? I know there's a saying that we should never ask, but let's make this exception."

"I'm nineteen." I'm thinking, *Damn! How did I go from being attracted to this woman, to feeling like a little ass kid?*

"Nine-teen!" she gasped. "Oh my God! What are y'all doing in a dangerous place like this by y'all selves? Don't you know this desert holds secrets! People that come here are never seen nor heard from again! That sand out there is like an ocean, but worse. Bodies don't surface here! You're just a baby."

I shook my head, "Hold on now. Whatchu mean *baby*? How old are you, if you don't mind me askin'?"

"I'm twenty-seven, sweety." She glanced out the window, then back at me. "But, you wouldn't believe the shit I've been through. I'm from the streets of Miami. They ain't no joke." She shook her head. "For some reason, I see a lot of me in you. You've lost someone. Who was it? And what happened to your neck?" She was concerned.

"I lost my mother when I was nine. Then, I ended up losing my sister!" I replied. "The scar on my neck is a long story."

"I'm sorry. That explains a lot. I couldn't imagine growing up without my mom. Then to lose my sister. I'm so, so sorry."

She patted my thigh. "You haven't healed. Sometimes we never do."

We ended up spending the remainder of our vacation partying with Sharnetta and her crew. She wanted to keep a close eye on us. They'd even convinced us into checking out of *The Luxor*. We grabbed a suite in the Mandalay Bay where they were staying. From The Venetian, Paris-Las Vegas, to the New York-New York, we'd hit all the best casinos. We cruised Lake Tahoe, and even went horseback riding. She spoke so highly of her husband and her little girl: Markeva. She taught me things I'd thought I'd already grasped, but truly had no clear understanding of. The strength of love and loyalty. Family, and being a woman. I learned so much from a complete stranger in such a short period of time, you'd think we'd known each other for years. I missed my mother and Shebba, and she now somehow reminded me of both. It was hard to say goodbye when it was time to part ways.

She'd given me a number to contact her, and said we were welcome in her home anytime. I'd reminded her that we're a group of six, and she'd only met two. She told me to bring them all. I'd extended the same invitation to the crib, but I'm hoping to be in something bigger before she took me up on it. She owns several properties. Some even had a guest house. It was time to head home. We hugged Sharnetta, JoVonna, Stephanie and Shonda tight, then boarded our flight.

Chapter 23

Weight

When I woke up, I was in a hospital bed. My head was wrapped like a mummy. My feet, what were left of them, felt like I had the worst case of athlete's feet known to man. My momma was sitting to my right. Though her eyes were closed, I could see she'd been in tears by the streaks they'd left beind. I didn't realize I'd been shot in the stomach until I tried to speak. A sharp pain ran from my nuts, through my stomach, all the way up to my chest. My throat was parched. I could see blood seeping through the sheets that oozed through the bandages wrapped around my feet and calves.

"Ma, ahem! Mama." I tried to raise my arm. Reaching in her direction, I realized something else. I was handcuffed to the bedrail.

"Oh! My baby's awake!" She rushed over to me. "I knew you would come back. You've been asleep for almost three weeks." She hugged me as far as her short arms could reach. She said, "They shotchu, busted ya head and burnt up ya feet. You done walked through hell before, ain'tcha?" She looked at me and smiled. A tear of anger rolled down my face.

I said, "Ma, I tried to—"

She said, "I know. I know, baby. You didn't wanna be it no more. You'd found God, and in Him you weren't of this world. But, let me tell you somethin'. If these folk want the *Weight* of this world on their shoulders! You give it to'em!" I nodded in agreement.

"You know ya parole officer is the one that found you? Emm-hmm! Strapped to a chair, shot, witcha feet still in the pot!" She rolled her eyes. She said, "Do you know that crazy white fool of a devil talkin' about revocating you! Yeah, baby, that's what she's talm bout." She fired up a square. Blowing out the smoke, she said, in her country drawl, "Yeah, she say she probably gon' send you back." She shook her head. I couldn't believe what I was hearing. I was fucked up! I hadn't harmed a soul, and they wanted to send me back for it. To the system, I'm just another number. Another dollar for the Department of Corrections. Yeah, I'd been through Hades. I'd met Satan himself, and a few of his minions. I swore when I'd left to never return, and that I'd hold court in the streets.

My momma said, "Some of your friends are here to see you. Their father couldn't stay, but they've been here everyday waiting on you to wake up. Let me step out here and get them and the nurse."

At first, I was thinking, fuck! These niggaz sticking around to finish the job! And now my momma involved. But, Moo and Doe stepped in. The first thing I said was, "Tell Teague, he gotta get me outta here."

Chapter 24

Teague

I know God probably looking down on me shaking His head right now. He'd brought me out of the fire. He'd blessed me with the love of my family, and had given me the opportunity to meet my fiancée, Athelia. As bad as I wanted to relax, coming home from the penitentiary, I couldn't rest. The situations with Hood and the twins brought me out of my state of dormancy. I had to find out exactly who these niggaz were that called themselves looking for me and mine. Knowing they intended to do bodily harm, I didn't have many options to choose from. I could only hope God understood that at times we're put in predicaments where it's *eat or be eaten*. In other words, it's kill or be killed. A rose that grew from the concrete, Athelia is a 32-year-old neurologist. Picturing her smile is what drives me to get out of bed in the morning. She's beautiful and bouji. As foxy as Ms. Pam Grier in her heydays, and a Beyoncé today. I don't wanna lose her. I can't. Though I hadn't exactly told her everything about me, she deserves to know the truth in this. Her life could very well be in danger. I couldn't risk her becoming a victim of my social familiarities. We were at her place. She'd prepared a delicious candlelight dinner for us. As she sat across the table from me, I was tense. I guess she sensed it, because I couldn't eat. She looked up at me with a perplexed expression on her face, as Marvin Gaye and Tammi Tarrell's duet—*You're All I Need To Get By*—played softly in the background. She's truly my sentiment of the classic.

Everything about this woman said: *grand ambition*.

"Baby, what's wrong? Is something wrong with the food?" she asked, setting her fork down.

"No-no-no. Not at all. It's good, babe. You've done your thing as always." I'd sliced another piece of the meatball from her Italian cuisine and put it in my mouth. "Mmmmm." I licked my lips, chewed and swallowed as she stared.

"Don't play with me, Corteague. What is it? You've been quiet all day. What's on your mind?"

"It's nothing, Athelia." I took a sip of my wine to wash the food down. She'd picked her fork back up, taking another bite as well. Now I was staring, admiring her beauty.

"Teague!" She pointed her utensil at me. "We lying now?" I expelled a sigh.

"A'ight, come here. Bring your wine, babe." I sat everything down. Dabbing the corners of my mouth with my handkerchief, I slid my chair back from the table. I love seeing her walk towards me. She's wearing an all-black Deo Volenté body dress, and now *Two Occasions* by The Deele floated through the dinning room as her anthem.

Giggling as I pulled her into my lap, she said, "Awwww, suki-suki now!"

"Ooh!" she cooed, making herself comfortable; she crossed her legs.

"What have I told you about trying to have your dessert before you've finished your dinner?" she asked, wrapping her arms around my neck, and kissing my lips.

"You love me?" I asked, looking into her eyes, caressing her thigh."

"Whatchu think?" she smiled.

"I'm serious now. Do you luh me unconditionally, no matter what?"

"Teague, you know I love you. Why do you ask?" she blushed and shrugged.

"I—I got something to tell you." Her smile faded.

"What, you cheatin'?" Her lips tightened.

"Hell n'aw Thei-Thei!"

"You're not having second thoughts, are you?" Her face showed concern.

"Nah, of course not. Look, you know about my past, right?"

"Some. What you've told me. I trust if there's something more out there that I should know about, you'd tell me. What's goin' on, Teague?"

"The street's callin' me, bae." I shook my head in dismay. I couldn't even look her in her eyes.

She frowned. Lifting my chin so my eyes met hers, she said, "So, answer that. Tell'em you chillin'! It"s that simple! You can't go back! We're about to get married, Corteague. You said you—"

"I know what I said. But this is shit that can't be avoided."

"Now I know damn well you ain't talkin' about sellin' no drugs! We got—"

"Hell muthafuckin' n'all! It's my kids, baby. Niggaz is comin' at my seeds. Listen, I need you to go be with your mother for a while."

"What? You want me to go to Detroit? Why?" She inclined her head.

"Shit could be dangerous for you around here, and—"

"I—I can't." She shook her head. "No!"

"Please, Athelia."

"Teague, you know I gotta work. You—"

"Listen, you said you had some vacation days coming up anyway."

"Em-mmm!" She took a sip of her wine. Taking it from her hand, I grabbed the wine glass by its stem and sat it on the table. She sighed.

"Please, queen. Look at me. I can't lose you to this game like I lost my first wife. This shit is serious. I need you gone like yesterday. I've just been waiting on the right time to tell you. You need to trust me on this."

"Okay, damn." She pouted in submission. "I guess I can talk to my boss tomorrow."

"And I was thinking. You've met Jah and Angela. I wanna see if my sons can convince them to get on outta here for a minute as well. Would you mind if they went with you?"

"Nah, it's cool. They're more than welcome to join me. It wouldn't be a problem. I've enjoyed their company. I'll call my momma tonight and let her know I'm coming."

"Please do."

"What about y'all though? You got me scared. Y'all gon' be all right?" she asked.

"We'll be fine. Don't worry. I'll make sure of it. And, thank you."

"No need. I love you." She stared into my gaze.

I grabbed my glass, raised it and handed her hers. "Let's toast."

"What are we toasting to?" she swirled her wine.

"To us. To true love."

"To true love." She held up her glass in salute. Clicking her wineglass to mine, we gulped until they both were empty. She took our glasses and sat them on the table.

"Now you gon' eat something? It's getting cold." Grabbing my knife and fork, she took some more meat and rolled some pasta onto the fork. Assuring she didn't spill anything and the sauce was just right, she fed me.

"Mmmm. Emm-hm." I chuckled as I chewed. "I'm gon' eat. Then I'll have my desert."

"Well, you better hurry up then, huh? It's moist, and chocolaty. Plus, you won't be able to have anymore for two long weeks." She purred, giving me a luring erotic smile. She said, "I've got cherries, strawberries and that whip cream that you like."

"Mmm, you do?" I smiled. "Chocolate syrup? You got some fudge?"

"Yup!" she replied, giving me that Gabrielle Union evil, but sexy grin.

"Well, we've got all night long to strawberry, chocolate-syrup and whip-cream it then, huh?"

"Ooh, don't forget the cherries. You like cherries, don'tchu?"

"I love cherries. And I don't wanna rush."

Chapter 25

AB

It was Christmas break, so I didn't have to go to school nor work. Keith Sweat's *Make It Last Forever* and the Tequila Sunrises we'd ordered had us feeling right as we sang along. I'd just given Ava a few quarters to go play us some *New Edition*. It was a cold Wednesday night. Me and my girls were bored, so we decided to head over to Sonny's to have a few drinks. Come to think of it, I should've left their asses at Chanel's, but I needed an alibi. We'd been there for about an hour when he came in with his Kango pulled low. I observed from a distance as he scanned the crowd. He was lookin' good in his quarter-length leather coat, black Lee jeans and black-on- black Adidas. I'd bought everything he had on, and he'd promised he'd wear them for our date tonight. He hadn't noticed me yet, but I was sure it wouldn't take him long to notice my entourage. Taliah, who puts you in the mind of Kelendria Rowland, was the first to say something as always. It wasn't surprising to me at all. I'd spun my bar stool around, giving everybody my back. I didn't wanna seem like I was jockin' a nigga when he looked our direction. However, I watched it all play out in the reflections of the mirrors in front of me. The melodies of *Can You Stand The Rain* drew a zeal from deep within as thoughts of our last escapade arose in my mind.

Taliah said, "Any, ooh girl! There go yo' friennnnd!" She smacked her lips and cocked her head to the side as she sized him up.

"Who?" I asked nonchalantly, as I sipped my drink.

My girl, Chanel, is the pro-black righteous type. She wears her hair natural, and she dresses very conservatively. She's woke. Meaning she's considered the conscious one out the clique. We all turn to her for answers when we've got a problem. Her love for our people seems to shine through everything she does, including how she speaks. Blessed with a lovely body, a chocolate skin tone, luscious lips and beautiful brown eyes, Ms. Revolutionary favors Lauryn Hill in her *Sister Act/Fugees* days.

She said, "Sistah, stop playin'. You see that king. And, em-em-mmm! He is fine!"

Trina li'l Toni Braxton-lookin' ass said, "Shit, don't look now. But here he come, bitch." She grinned, as N.E.'s *If It Isn't Love* burst forth from the speakers. A Chrisette Michele lookalike, Ava didn't say anything, which was odd. She just looked at me with her eye brows raised. Even though she'd stood silent, I told her ass to shut up. I could read her mind.

The oversized gold dookie rope around his neck looked as if it weighed a ton. Representing power, respect, as well as where he's from, his diamond-encrusted medallion hung to the middle of his stomach. The piece swung like a pendulum with his swagger as he approached us. I stood and turned around to greet him. He smelled so good in his *Michael Jordan* cologne. And oh, me? Picturing me in your mind's eye, you could say Ashanti when you think about how I looked. She could probably do me in a movie portrayal.

Taliah said, "Damn, you ain't gon' even let him sit down?" I didn't even respond. I just took him by the hand, pulling him to the side.

"Hey, you. You're late." I smiled, leading him away from my crew. I ain't need them all in my business.

"Sorry, baby. Something came up that I had to take care of. You still with me tonight or what? I left the car runnin' so I could keep the heat blowin'. Cold as it is, a nigga gotta keep that shit pumpin'." He blew into his fist.

"Yeah. Let me let them know I'm leaving. Hold up." Though some of my girls thought some of my moves were kinda suspect lately, they hadn't a clue I'd been seeing him on the low for a while. With all the lies to my momma, my friends and my man, things were becoming hard to juggle. I hid it well. So I thought. I walked back over to the bar, trying to keep a straight face as I conjured up the first fib.

"Hey-hey, y'all. Im'a gonna go get somethin' to eat wit—"

"Wasuuup, bitch? We see you goin' Moo tonight!" Taliah cut me off mid-sentence, posting her hand on her hips.

Giving me a wry grin, Ava said, "I knew yo' sneaky ass was up to somethin'!"

"I—I, I ain't doin' nothin'. We just gon' go—"

"Stop lying, girl, and just go." Chanel shooed me.

Trina said, "Em-hmm. You must think we stupid or somethin'? We see the way you look at that nigga when he come around."

"King! Not *nigga*, my love!" Chanel interjected.

"What-ever." Trina waved her off. "Gon' get outta here. We'll cover for if 'you know who' ask any questions as always. How long has it been now y'all?"

"Uh-unn! How long have y'all bitches known?" I asked. I was laughing, but it was derisive. I couldn't argue. I was cold busted.

"We'll talk about that later." Ava smiled, giving me googly eyes. After an awkward moment of silence, we'd all agreed that we'd spent the night Chanel's before I left. It was a relief to know my girls had me. I told them I'd be back by 4 a.m. We had to travel a good distance not to be seen. After dinner, we caught a movie. We went to see Spike Lee's *Do the Right Thing*, which was ironic under the circumstances. Moo had his hands all over me, causing us to miss more than half the movie.

Chapter 26

Lose Control

The next thing I knew, we were at the Fairfield Inn, which was the nearest hotel. The heat was on. Sweat sheathed my body as my juices ran down my thighs. I tried my best to bury my screams of pleasure, but I couldn't.

He'd sucked my pussy so good, I made sounds I didn't even know I was capable of. Now he had my face down in the mattress, ass up, slowly stroking my love cave. And though I knew it was wrong, it felt so good.

"Ah! Ohhh!" I screamed into the pillow as his balls slapped against my skin each time he drove deep inside me.

"I wanna hear you," he whispered, increasing his pace. He knew I'd eventually have to come up for air. I didn't want whomever might be next door to think I'm a freak if they happened to see us leaving.

I'd held back as much as I could. He snatched the pillow from me. Looking back at him with ecstasy in my eyes as I reached for the pillow seemed to arouse him even more. Gripping my hips, he was swaying his, thrusting against my walls so much that I'd lost control.

"Ooohhh! Moo-moozeeeere!" I couldn't believe he had me yellin'. "This pussy yours! Ahh-Ahh!"

"What? Whatchu say?" he asked, talking dirty to me.

"This-yo-puss-saaay!" I screamed, throwin' it back at him. He had my ass in every position humanly possible, making me explode over and over again. When we finally yielded to temptation, it was so powerful. We were both out of breath after fuckin' like two wild beasts for almost two hours.

"Whoo! Boy, yo' black ass can fuck!" I told him as I laid in his arms gasping for air.

"I know," he replied with a smile.

"A'ight. Don't get big-headed now." I kissed his lips.

"Whatchu think about what I asked you on our way here?" he asked.

"What? As far as me goin' outta town with Athelia and Jah because some beef or whatever?"

"Yeah. Whatchu gon' do? Jah with it."

"I don't know." I shrugged.

"Whatchu mean you don't know? You know what happened to Jah when—"

"I know, Moo, but damn! What we supossed to do in Detroit cold as it is? You know Christmas and the New Year comin'?"

"Y'all can do the same shit you'd do here. Go shopping or somethin'. At least I'd know you're safe. You need to make a decision. I told them I'd have an answer tonight."

"A'ight, a'ight. I guess I'll go if you want me to. I'm coming home for the holidays though." He kissed me.

"That's what I wanted to hear."

"I just don't know what Im'a say."

"You'll come up with somethin'. You ready for round two?" he asked.

"Em-hmm. I ain't never ran from a challenge." I smiled.

"Well, come here then. It's your turn." He pulled me on top of him. We'd made love so passionately, that we both fell asleep afterwards. I was awakened by the constant buzz and rattle of his pager going off in the drawer of the nightstand. I'd gotten up to use the bathroom. I had to pee bad! Gazing at the clock, it was somehow flashing 12:00 a.m. After using the bathroom and washing my hands, I came out. Walking over to the window, I opened the curtains. My reaction was like that of a vampire caught by the morning's sun rays. *Shit!* I thought to myself.

"Moo-Moo! Moo, get up! What time is it?" I panicked, knowing I was supposed to have been back at Chanel's hours ago. He rolled over. I slid my lace panties on. I was now jumpin' up and down, trying to squeeze into my jeans. "I gotta go, boy! Getcho ass up! Look, the sun is out!"

He sat up and smiled.

"I don't see shit funny!"

He had the nerve to mumble that the sun comes out everyday.

"Get dressed!" I grabbed a pillow and flung it at'em. "You make me—Ooh! Where my bra at?"

"I don't know. It's around here somewhere. What happened to the clock?" He stretched.

"I was hoping you could tell me."

He opened the drawer of the nightstand and grabbed his pager and both of his guns.

"Damn, It's 11:07. I gotta call Pops nem. Him and bro been blowin' me up."

"You still sittin' there! Get dressed!"

"I am. Stop buggin'," he replied, giving me a dismissive look. I rolled my eyes as he reached for the phone. I'd found my bra, and he was staring as I put it on.

"Whatchu lookin' at?" I threw my U.W.M sweater over my head and headed for the bathroom to fix my hair, wash my face and brush my teeth. By the time I got out, I was thanking God he was off the phone and had gotten dressed. Tucking one gun in the front of his pants, and the other at the small of his back, he was ready. He grabbed his coat, then handed me mine.

"You sure you don't want me to go warm the car up before we go?" he asked.

"N'all, we gotta go. It'll warm up on the way. Are you just gon' leave all those rubbers on the floor?" I frowned.

"Shit, that's what they pay housekeepers for." He smirked, pulled out a wad and threw a hundred-dollar bill on bed.

"Em-mmmm! You just? I'm gon' have to teach you some manners." I turned my nose up, shaking my head. "Don't even trip. I got it."

I went in the bathroom and gathered a clot of toilet paper and scooped up the condoms that were strewn about. I hadn't realized we'd used six. I flushed them and washed my hands again.

"Now, come-mo!" I told him as I waltzed out the bathroom towards the door.

We were finally on our way to the car.

"You sweated my hair out. It's a mess!" I shoved him playfully as we walked the corridor towards the exit.

"It ain't my fault. You better tell that nigga you were dancing, or you got into a fight or some shit." He chuckled.

"You real funny. You know that?"

"You didn't think I was funny last night. Now, did you? If that's my pussy then—" he paused.

"Then what, crazy?" I asked as we stepped outside. Moo suddenly stopped and reached for his waist. When I looked up and saw Boomer getting out of his truck, I froze. With my breath caught in my throat, I felt wobbly.

"Angie, bring yo' mutha-fuckin' ass here!" he yelled. I stepped out from behind Moo. Crossing my arms, I walked towards my heart. He was looking at me with such disgust, I could see his soul within his eyes.

"I'm sorrrry!" I pled.

"A.B., you good?" Moo asked, gun in hand. I looked back and nodded. My boyfriend answered for me as well, as he shoved me in the driver's seat of the truck and slammed the door.

"Yeah, she good! Fuck you mean, nigga?"

"A'ight now. You heard what the fuck I said. Watch that tone, my nigga. She better be!" Moo warned him as Boomer walked around to the passenger side and hopped in. I pulled off.

Chapter 27

Doe

'The more things change, the more they stay the same.' That's some strange dichotomy for you, ain't it? I can't tell you if the saying is true, or even true-ish. Pops say, back in the day, the Mil was more organized. He said we had our own black syndicate. Today, it's more divided and the weak are concurred. We block bang. It's every hood for itself, so it's definitely not the same. You can easily identify what a nigga representing by color. Nigga reppin' 2-7 rock that Philadelphia 76'ers shit. Hillside niggaz sport the Raiders attire. While gangstaz like myself fucks with the Georgetown and the Duke Blue Devils. The list goes on. That being said, me and bruh were trying to convince Teague that it wouldn't be a problem finding these niggaz, eat-n'em and getting'em gone. However, for reasons of his own, he wanted the big homey—Weight—out the hospital before we commenced to wreckin' shit. Being we'd only known him since he's been home, we were skeptical to his character. So, Teague told us a story or two about their time together in the Feds. The locale and origin of their story started in a USP.

***

Terre Haute, United States Penitentiary. The maximum facility is based in the great state of Indiana. It was the first joint Teague landed in during his journey. It's also where he'd met Weight. Pops quickly explained the distinction relating to State and Federal penal institutions. He basically said, depending on where you were housed, a state penitentiary could be considered one in the same as a daycare center in comparison to a USP. In the feds, the geographic structures are distinguished by what they call 'Cars'. In other words, the joints are sectioned off by groups. You've got a West Coast Car, a East Coast Car, Midwest, D.C. and etcetera. Different Cars also consist of different gangs. You got the Folks, Vice Lords, Kings, Bloods, Crips, Muslim, Christians, and so forth. When you come through the doors, you're screened and directed as to whatever state or region of the world you're from. Pops being from the Mil, he was directed towards the grounds where Midwest niggaz held it down. Being a gangsta, he got up with that Car as soon as he dropped his property off at his cell. It doesn't take long to find out who's-who's in the feds. With the MOB you had a two-week grace period to produce your paperwork, or you had to move around.

If your shit came back and you were solid, you were good. Anything to the contrary of what's considered a 'real nigga', a severe beating was gettin' off light.

The possibility of death loomed in your immediate future. A lil' nigga out of Chicago they called Shorty had the joint, and he didn't play no games. The only optional means of escape was to be 'ran up top'. This is the term used when one would alert the authorities in order to check out a unit. You were then taken into protective custody. Pops valid, so he was more than welcomed. Weight was his celly. Being they're both from Milwaukee, they jammed off top. Weight was "Hardhead' off 24th in Capitol. At 34 years old, he'd been down ten years on a fifteen-year sentence for a Reckless and Cocaine Distribution. He'd served his time in the state, and was finishing the remainder of his term in the feds. He'd heard stories about Teague out in the world gettin' money. He'd also heard about the body and the indictment against him before he'd made it to trial.

To be aware is to be alive. So, puttin' Pops on everything he needed to know as far as the bid was his first mission. Long before they'd arrived, the institution was dubbed 'Terror Haute."

This is due to its atrocities. Holding terrorists, killers, serial murderers, rapists and drug dealers, it's deemed one of the most dangerous prisons in the United States. Without measure or degree, it was the norm when it came to inmates being murdered. This was so regular; it didn't take Teague long to witness just how hellish the clink really was.

Chapter 28

Sturdy

Three days into his bid, he and Weight were up on 3D in their cell, preparing a meal, when they heard a tap on the door. It was one of the guys. A black ass nigga with a mouthful of gold they called St. Louis. Weight gave him the nod, and he'd stepped in.

"What up, my niggaz!" he said, showing them some love, "Weight, I just got word from Shorty. The young boy Tug ain't paid back that money, he done went to every Car in this mutha-fucka borrowin' to feed that gambling habit. You know what time it is." St. Louis folded his arms, and waited on Weight's response.

He sighed, shaking his head. "It's been months. How much the lil' nigga owe?" he asked, slicing and dicing a Halal meat, as Teague shredded the cheese and peppers.

"He owe us fifty-five hundred. Ain't no telling how much he owe the other Cars."

The Mob had six hitters that moved in twos when it came to collecting dues. He and St. Louis were their top two butchers. When Shorty sent for'em, there were no other options on the table. Death was literally around the corner.

"Where he at?" Weight asked.

"He in his cell. PDG down there rattlin' with him now. His bunkie on a visit. He under arrest, and don't even know it."

Weight said, "You relieved on this one. I'll take Teague with me to stand on security. Just hold the tier. When you see us comin', pull PD outta there."

"You sure G?"

"Positive. It's personal. I know his people. Head on down there. We on our way to take care of it right now."

"A'ight, I'm gon'." St. Louis left.

"Teague, wrap everything up you got over there until we get back. This should only take a few minutes."

"Who is this nigga Tug?" Teague asked as Weight put on extra layer of his state attire. He'd always stashed extras specifically for situations such as this one.

"A nigga out the hood. He's one of mine, but ain't nothin' I can do for'em. He jammed. It's too much money. I ain't got it. His people ain't got it either, so ain't no checkin' out. That would leave the burden on me, and I've warned him. I guess he thought this shit was a game."

He pulled a twelve-inch shiv he'd hidden from the lining of the stainless steel toilet. Tearing a piece of his sheet, he wrapped his right hand. Tearing another piece, he enwrapped the end of the knife so he could grip it.

He said, "All you need to do is, stand outside the cell and make sure don't nobody else come in. He's one tier below us. Follow me?" Though Teague was nervous, he nodded in agreement. Walking out of the cell, they moved swiftly towards their destination. Though the dayroom was packed, other convicts were preoccupied with various games like Chess, Dominos and Spades. Others were on the phone, or watching TV.

Coming down the stairs, they saw St. Louis standing outside a cell in the middle of the cellblock. The door to the cell was cracked about three quarters of an inch. As they approached, he called PDG out, and Weight slid in. Pops said all he heard was Tug's plea.

"Hold on! Weight, I—" Then the gruesome sounds of flesh being pierced, and bones being crushed by the sturdy steel knife manufactured from a support bracket of an old bunk frame. When Weight was sure Tug was dead, he grabbed a bath towel that hung on a hook in the back of the cell and wiped the blood from his face, arms and his hands. He then took off the outer layer of blood-spattered clothing. Using the knife, he shredded the blood-soaked clothes and flushed them down the toilet. This was one of many stories about Teague and the big homey Pops shared with us at the hospital as we patiently waited for him to come to. By his account, Weight was a savage with the knives behind the walls. Before his incarceration, there was also a point in time where he was said to be barbaric behind the artillery. After hearing about his personage, I personally wanted to see what Big O.G. was all about. I wondered if he still possessed that gangsterism at heart we'd heard tales of. The man we'd met had changed. Some called him a Bible thumper. Hopefully he can come up outta that jam.

Chapter 29

Weight
-Ecclesiates 3:3

In the hospital, the inexplicable voices in my heart and mind strive against one fold. Clearly, the Lion, Alpha, Omega, True and Faithful and King of Kings was in my right ear. Beelzebub, Apollyon, Old Scratch and Lucifer invaded the other. The Lamb repeatedly told me, "Peace, be still. I will never leave nor forsake you." Beguiled by the hollow stalk of the Prince of Darkness, reminding me of the 30 years I faced heading back to prison. Vivid images of things I've endured behind the wall flashed before my eyes. I felt the despair, agony, pain, suffering and torment I'd felt in the joint right there as I laid cuffed to the bed. Being desolate, dependant, surrounded by grief and misery, was something I never wanted to feel again. Belial thrived on these weaknesses, and used these ambiances to exploit rationalism buried deep within. Though the Lord of Lords whispered, "I too have once felt all these things", the callous rings overlaying my heart stilted my mind. The Bright Morning Star said unto me, "To know these rigorous tribulations, is to know the road Erebus without the Son of Man." The Holy Spirit warned me not to turn from Him, but I'd come to a decision. Unfaltering, I'd decided I'd greet death with open arms before returning to the melancholy of a prison cell.

No longer in the ICU, I'd been placed on an 8th floor recovery wing. Due to high-tech surveillance system recently installed, Teague would only go so far in aiding me in my escape. He'd provided the tools, but it would be up to me to make it to the parking lot. A police officer being posted outside my room around-the-clock, and Froedert being as big as it is, my timing has to be precise and unerring. Sliding the Bobby pin out of my mouth, I removed the handcuff restricting my right arm. Cuffing a syringe filled with eight cc's of Succinylcholine, I crept out of bed. Though it pained me, I managed to hide my bulky frame behind the door.

The nurse doing her 3 a.m. walkthrough never knew what hit her as she stepped inside. Grabbing her from behind, I snatched her off her feet, forcefully injecting the coup de grace into the side of her neck. Covering her mouth so she couldn't scream, I held her tight as the muscle relaxer took effect, causing her body to slump. She went limp. Asking God for forgiveness, I slowly laid her on the floor, shedding a tear for her soul. She'd been nice to me during my stay and hadn't deserved such punishment. But time was of the essence. My window was closing. Within the next two-hundred and forty minutes, my Parole Officer's motif to Hallmark State Property across my back brought a qualm within that is beyond repose. Looking down at Ms. Cerol, there wouldn't be any waking up. I'd been told the injection would cause her to have a heart attack. She's dead, and there's no turning back.

I cursed myself for leaving her kids without a mother. Sneaking out of the hospital undetected would be difficult. My once wiry frame now said six-foot-seven and three-hundred and twenty pounds. I had to move fast, and with a precipitant flow. Taking a quick peek outside the room, the officer on duty was preoccupied with a crossword puzzle and looked as if he was barely awake. Ripping him from the chair, I pulled him inside. With the tip of his loafer scurrying across the linoleum floor, he grasped for his holster to no avail. Choking him with one hand, I grabbed his weapon with the other tossing it aside.

"I'm sorry! But I ain't goin' back," I whispered as I applied pressure to his neck. Gripping his throat with both hands, I'd crushed his windpipe, strangling him to death.

"I hope you ain't got no kids," I told the lifeless corpse. Laying him on the floor, I closed his eyes. Though the uniform would be a snug fit, it would have to do. After changing clothes, I dragged the bodies into the bathroom. Catching a glimpse of my reflection in the mirror caused me to pause. I stopped and stared. I hadn't groomed myself in months. My beard and mustache have grown wild. My eyes are bloodshot from the tears. The dreads hanging past my shoulders look more like a wool mop. Sadly, I recognize the cacodemon staring back at me. The animal in me has resurfaced.

Chapter 30

Forlorn

Stepping outside the room to my left, I heard the colloquy of the other females at the nurses' station down the hall. I could also smell the aroma of freshly brewed coffee. Instead of heading their direction and causing more demise in an attempt to board the elevator, I headed right, exiting the door leading to the stairwell. When I got to the bottom, peering through the door, I scanned the lobby. If I'd stepped into the vestibule, freedom lay less than 20 feet away. However, the lobby wasn't quiet clear as I'd hoped it would be. There were two more of Milwaukee's finest standing at the desk, talking with the female receptionist. All of them were white. Looking down at the gun in my hand, I weighed my options. "Shit!" I scoffed. I wanted to leave quietly as possible. I was barefooted. The dead cop's shoes hadn't fit, and the socks would surely cause me to lose grip if I had to run. Wearing tight highwater pants, and a shirt where the sleeves clearly didn't fit, there was no way I could simply walk out unnoticed. Pounding my forehead with my fist, I'd decided I'd have to chance making another exit on another wing. I headed back up, and East.

***

Meanwhile, a few stories above me, Selena's best friend—Sonia discovered—the carnage I'd left behind.

Screaming, she slowly backpedaled out of the room. Backing into the hallway, she'd hit the wall and slid down on her butt.

"Th-they're dead! They're deeead! Seleeeeena!" she cried as others rushed to her side.

"What's-the-matter?" Fionna, their shift supervisor, asked as she approached the gathering crowd.

"Sel-Selena!" Sonia pointed towards the room.

Fionna cautiously walked in the room to see an empty bed, with a pair of handcuffs dangling from its rail. A faint foul smell caused her to look to her left to see the bone chilling sight of the two bodies stuffed in the small enclosure, lying atop of each other. She got her black ass up outta there immediately.

The radio was silent. If they were on to me, I'd know their every move. Walking past an old man on the 3rd floor, paranoia caused me to start sweating profusely. The nurse paid me no mind, but the old black man raked me from head to toe, giving me a suspicious look. He'd definitely noticed that I wasn't wearing any shoes. Suddenly, an alarm sounded. A male voice came over the PA system.

"Attention, Security and all personnel! We've got an officer down on the 8th floor. I repeat! We have an officer down! A prisoner has escaped! Be on the lookout for an African American, approximately 6'8 and three-hundred pounds! The suspect is to be considered armed and dangerous. He's likely to be impersonating a police officer. Seal all exits!"

***

In the lobby, the veteran of the two officers barked orders.

"I'm going up! Call it in, we need back up! Make sure nobody gets on or off those elevators! I'm taking the stairs to the right!" The other officer ordered the security guard to cover the stairwell to the left as he called for reinforcements.

Gun in hand, I took flight, running towards the stairwell leading to my nearest exit. I'd hit the door and sprinted down the stairs. I'd made it, but the door wouldn't open. It had been secured from the inside somehow.

Hearing footsteps advancing in my direction from below, I opened fire, causing the glass door to shatter. Diving through, sliding on my back across the shards of glass, I rolled to my feet. The radio chatter was no longer silent as it was seconds prior.

"We've got shots fired in the East stairwell! Shots fired! Proceed with caution!"

Running fast as my injured feet would take me across the the frozen blacktop, I had to make it back to the front of the hospital where a car awaited me. The morning air bit at me, as the cold air filled my lungs. I felt weak, slow and dizzy. I hadn't calculated the brazen fact that being off my feet for so long would have such great effect on my body.

With each stride, my feet lost skin and began to bleed. Heart racing in my chest, lungs flaring, I didn't stop. Sirens swelled in the distance, as the blare of the hospital's horns polluted any promise of peace to the ill suffering on this dark side of dawn. I rounded the building, and, as promised, a white Fleetwood sat idling in the handicap zone. Two old women were inside. The trunk popped as I approached. I opened it and dove inside. I hadn't closed the trunk all the way when I heard a police cruiser come to a rest next to the car. The radio came to life.

"We've got a visual at the—"

Knowing I'd been spotted, I rose back up, sending a hail of gunfire into the vehicle, killing the two men inside. The Cadillac's wheels slowly revolved as I tucked myself inside the trunk. I was officially on the run.

About twenty minutes later, when the trunk finally opened, we were in a 24-hour parking garage downtown on Wisconsin Avenue. Taking off their wigs, the two ladies I'd thought were senior citizens when I'd gotten in were actually young and beautiful. One had a cinnamony skin tone. Her naturally curly hair, brown eyes and radiant smile said *Rachel True* all day. She said, "Took you long enough! We almost left yo' ass. Anyway, hey. I'm Telesis."

The other had a complexion like banana sunshine. She was a tiny little something, but beautiful as well. Looking like the one and only Jada P., she said, "What up? I'm Honesty."

Opening the back door on the driver's side, she grabbed a duffle bag and tossed it to me as Telesis doused the Lac with gasoline.

"You's a big dude. Damn, Teague and the Twins said you were tall, but you're huge!" Lesis lit a cigarette and threw the match, igniting the flame as we walked away from the car. Telesis turned to me as we strolled.

She said, "I wish we had more time to get acquainted, but we don't. Here." She threw me a set of keys and pointed to our right. "Those are to the black Thunderbird over there with the tinted windows. It's clean and gassed up. In the bag, you've got yourself fifty-thousand in cash. There's also a change of clothes, some shoes, and two Colt Commanders in that bitch."

"Don't forget the ID's," Honesty reminded her.

"Oh yeah. There's a bunch of fake ID's and socials in there too. Teague said hit that line. You know the number. We'll be seeing you around. Honesty, let's roll." The ladies walked away.

With no time to waste, I jogged over to the Pontiac and jumped in. The tires shrieked as I burned rubber, pulling out of the parking spot. Pulling alongside them, I rolled the window down.

"Hey, thank y'all. A'ight."

As we heard the gas tank on the Lac explode, I looked back momentarily. "You good. We got paid, my dude." Telesis smiled.

"Believe dat!" Honesty said. Throwing up 3C, she gave me a salute. "Girl, you see his feet?" she asked Telesis.
I smashed out.

Chapter 31

Moo

Jahnahdah and Athelia were gone. I hadn't been able to get back in touch with A.B. before they left. She'd called and let me know what happened, and exactly how we got caught up. Not hearing from her had me all fucked up. Apparently, one of Boomer's cousins worked at the hotel. As we checked in, she'd recognized A.B. from their family reunion she'd accompanied him to some months prior. I'd thought the lady was looking at me crazy, but I paid it no mind. Now, it's Tuesday morning. Space heater ablaze, me, Doe and Jilla were at the spot on Center standing around the table in the basement. We were bussin' down and baggin' a few bricks. Knowing the fiends would be out in droves soon, we were tryin' to get shit together before the sun rose.

"So, whatchu think, bruh?" I looked at Doe.

"About what? Gettin' these old-ass walls sealed so we can hold some heat in this mu-fucka?" He knew what I was talking about. He was just fuckin' with me. For the past 48 hours, all I'd been talking about was A.B.

"Hell n'aw. About Angie. You think she still fuckin' with me?" He laughed at me, even though he knew he shouldn't have. He knew my position.

"Wasup, Moo? I know you ain't in love? She got a nigga! It's been what, a couple days? You actin' like you ain't seen the girl in weeks!" Doe replied.

"Stop playin'. You know better." I pursed my lips to the side.

Jilla said, "I don't know, homeboy. Ever since she put that pussy on you, you have been actin' different."

"Fuck-you-mean *different*, nigga?" I scoffed.

"What I mean is Maya fine ass was basically throwin' that pussy at you the other night. You gotcha head so far up this bitch's ass, I bet you didn't even notice.

Maya James is super bad! Not taking nothin' from Angie. But I'm talkin' 5'5, chocolate skin tone and a smile like Lupita's. Body of a goddess, thick! Ass like Serena's. I had to be sick.

Doe said, "What! Maya tryna give you that pussy and you frontin'? Did you at least get the number? Please, tell me you got the digits."

I said, waving him off, "Maaan, that skizza."

"Huh? I didn't hear you! Go-head, finish that sentence. That skizza what? That skizza what, huh? I wanna hear this!" He looked at me sideways. I dropped my head. I couldn't say shit, because I knew he was right. Not only is she beautiful, her reputation is solid.

Doe said, "You know what? I ain't surprised." He taunted me. "Mm-hmm. I know what it is, my nigga. She put that voo-doo-ooh-ooh on yo' ass! Held out on that good shit, then pow! Now that she done unleashed that wet-wet, she gotcho fool ass stuck." He laughed.

"Just like Jah got my ass."

"You a'ight?" Jilla said.

"I'm straight. I jus—"

"Pussy whiiiiped!" they both teased in unison.

Doe said, "Shit, you don't wanna give Maya no play? She can be part of my team. I'll gladly hit that."

"Somebody need to hit her. This nigga trippin'. He need a cigarette." Jilla laughed.

"Yeah, right. What team? You ain't cheatin' on Jah. And you! You'll stick yo' dick in yo' cousins. I know you ain't talkin'."

Jilla said, "If she ain't never spent the night at my Granny's and she fine, that ass can get it. But, this ain't about me. Maya ain't no kin to you, boy! You better stop playin'. I'll have that ass up in the spot for two-three weeks! Doin' nothin' but nuttin'! Doe, get this fool."

"You right. I haven't been cheatin' on Jah. But, she's outta town. Plus, I ain't gon' fuck her. You is. She wouldn't know the difference. Let me catch her fine ass slippin'. Doppelgang that ass. You know how we do it."

I laughed, "Damn, foolie! We did used to get'em cold, huh?"

"Hell yeah. You wanna bring it back on'em?"

Jilla said, "Y'all gon' pull it fa-real?"

Doe said, "Nah, I'm just bullshittin'. You know I can't cheat on the light of my life. I'm just tryna cheer this nigga up."

"Moo, don't worry. She gon' call you, my nigga. Then you can have your way with her right over there on the pool table." Jilla chuckled.

"Y'all got jokes," I replied, giving a ghost of a smile.

"Nah, fa-real though. On some real shit, you gon' be a'ight. You gotta be. You're about to be an uncle." Doe tied a knot in a baggie, throwing another once across the table. "Jah pregnant."

I said, "Whaaaat! Wh-why you playin'! Ha-haaaa! You bullsittin!" Rushing around the table, I scooped him off his feet. He knew that would make me smile. Jilla congratulated him as well after I'd released my bear hug. We were elated in receiving the good news of adding a new edition to the family. After packaging everything up, we headed out to celebrate Doe becoming a father.

Chapter 32

Hood
4:30 a.m.

We'd all agreed it was time. Dressed in white mechanic jumpers and Michael Myers masks, we were heading in on our next lick. Tonight's target was the blue dope house in the middle of 10th in Atkinson.

It's snowin' hard as a bitch out here! This punk-ass blizzard makin' it hard for me to see! A dog barkin' to my left got me on edge. Checkin' our surroundings, I ain't see shit but a cat scurrying across the alley. I turned my attention back towards the house. It's quiet, as so it seems. I'm knowin' that's just a facade. Behind that side door stands a nigga holdin' a AK-47 or something just as deadly. With him, there's roughly six more niggaz in there. All of'em strapped. These niggaz don't play. But shit, neither do we. All the footprints in the snow tells me it's been a busy night for the 'Dime Bag Crew'. They move all the small shit like fifties, balls, quakers, and halves from the first floor. The second floor holds the zips and the splits. These niggaz keep the bricks and the money in the attic. So, we want one floor. The top!

I got this fat hype bitch we snatched up on her way here in front of me on her knees, with .45 to the back of her cranium. This hoe scared shitless. She shakin' like Don Knotts. I let Lue talk to her, 'cause I ain't got the patience. She dead anyway. We can't let her go, and we can't risk tryin' to keep an eye on her while we go in. She's a threat to security. She gots'-ta-go!

Lue said, "Listen, calm down, bitch. All you gotta do is knock how you usually knock, and ask for who you always ask for. If anything was to go down because of yo' ass, I'm killiin' you first. Understand? Now, who you come to see?"

"T-T-T-Dog! I ju-just came to cop from T-Dog! I needed me a ball!"

"Shhhh! Calm down. Shut-cho-ass up!" Lue scolded her. What she didn't know was, we knew exactly who was in there movin' the product. If she would've attempted to lie, or say the wrong name, we would've killed her ass right there. But, she was being truthful. I took over from there.

I said, "A'ight, getcho ass up!" I threw up four fingers, then Lue, Sweets, Mula and Bri went ahead of us, taking their positions on the side of the house. The front door of the spot was barricaded. We'd done our homework. It's never used. Any and everything in or out this muthafucka comes out this one door, or this back window. This bitch was our ticket in.

Moo and Doe criminal-minded asses done somehow came up with a way to make silencers out of Styrofoam and shoe boxes. The shit actually works! They only fit the Macs, though. The rest of us goin' in as is. Mula grabbed one of the Macs to give Lue some assistance. Hopefully, they'll be doing all the shootin' if it goes up. Otherwise, shit gon' get real hectic.

I said, "What's ya name?"

She said, "Sheila."

"Sheila, you got kids?"

"Yeah. I-I got five of'em," she replied.

"Well, I'd advise you to knock like you love'em then. Knock!" I whispered in her ear. She knocked in code, hitting the door with two taps, and a pound.

"Who dat!" a man's voice could be heard coming from the other side of the door.

"Sheila! Packman, it's me—Sheila!" I'm thinking to myself: *Yeah, he a killa*. I've heard of this nigga. I could hear the locks clicking. He opened up and looked at Sheila though the iron bars on the secure screen door. He then unlocked and opened it as well. As soon as he did that, Lue put rounds in him and Sheila. I had to catch Packman big ass before he hit the ground. Heavy bastard fell right in my arms. He had an automatic shotgun sittin' next to the door frame. We let Sheila flop her big ass right there in the blanket of snow. We had to get in, and get out!

"Four minutes," I told the team, as I handed Sweets the shotty. Me, Mula and Bri went up, while Lue and Sweets held it down outside. Inside the stairwell, behind door number one on the first floor, we heard music, and niggaz laughin' and talkin' shit. This lick was way overdue. My brothers used to help run this bitch some years back. These dumb ass niggaz still using the knock codes from back then. Once bruh 'nem found out about that, they felt niggaz deserved to be touched. We were tryna walk as light as possible, but shit! These are some creaky-ass steps. The second floor was quiet as hell. Before I hit the attic door with the code, I stepped to the side just in case.

After three pounds and two taps, we could hear footsteps descend in our direction. Two clicks, the door opened.

Mu let the Mac talk. We couldn't risk the nigga making a sound. His body jerking and jolting from the slugs, he'd dropped his gun. I tried to catch him, but his body fell backwards and hit the steps with a loud thud as I grasped his T-shirt. On top of that, the loud thumps his cannon made when it landed and tumbled down the steps was loud as a bitch too! Shit! We paused. Movement could be heard behind door number two. Somebody was unlocking the door. I looked at Bri and Mula, giving them the signal to exercise their right to bear arms while I grabbed the bricks and the money. Looks like we'd have to do a lil' more killin' than expected. Fuck'em!

Chapter 33

Mula

As soon as the door cracked, I opened fire, sending rounds straight through that bitch. When I stopped shooting, all we heard was a body drop, and what sounded like a gun hittin' the floor. We struggled to push the door open. *Fuck, this nigga done fell against the door?* I thought to myself. We entered the kitchen of the upstairs apartment, guns up. These dudes had it lookin' more like a fully equipped laboratory. Paraphernalia, dope, pots, scales and boxes of Arm & Hammer were littered carelessly about. A nigguh the streets knew as Boomer laid stretched out in a pool of his own blood. Laying next to him was a .41 revolver. I picked that chunky muthafucka up, cuffing it under my armpit. Shit, now we gotta clear this bitch. Making our way through the kitchen, directly to our right is a bathroom. It's empty. In front of us is a bedroom door that's closed. I looked at Bri, countin' down with my fingers. I made sure she understood we were going in on three. One—two—three! We barged in pointing our weapons in every direction. The room looked as if it was empty. I checked the closet and under the bed while Bri covered me. It was clear.

Moving from there, we entered the living room, which was empty as well. Wasn't shit in there, but a run-down sofa, a TV, which was on. A Nintendo system, some games and its controls were scattered about.

From the looks of it, we'd interrupted a nigguh's game of Contra. He had the game paused. *Shit, game over, nigguh*, I thought to myself. There was one more room towards the front of the living room. Moving slowly and cautiously, we listened. We heard nothing. I looked at Bri, and again I held up three fingers. One—two—three! I twisted the knob and pushed the door open. We saw no one. We heard movement coming from the kitchen area. Glancing over my shoulder, I saw that Bri had her gun trained in that direction. I turned my head for a split second to see Hood bend the corner, coming towards us in her bloody jumper. Her duffle bags were filled to their capacity. A smile stretched across my face beneath my mask. She tapped her watch, and clapped her hands twice. "Time!" I noticed that she looked at the TV screen, and then back at us. Something was wrong! The closet door in the bedroom swung open as I stood in the doorway. When I turned to look, all I saw was the flash. The impact threw me off balance. I'm falling. Bri opened fire with her twins. I feel like—like the winds been knocked outta me. I–I can't catch my breath.

"Mulaaaaah!" I heard her scream. I'm thinking, *Damn Hood! I hear you! Hold up. I need to catch my—Catch my breath.* As I'm lyin' on the floor, I see Hood's feet rush to my side. She rolled me over on my back and took off my mask.

"Mulaah!"

In my head I'm saying, *I'm a'ight. I see you, Sis.* She stood up bussin' her guns in the direction in which she'd just came. I hear multiple gunshots being fired. I'm—I'm losing consciousness. *Fuck! This muthafucka done shot me.*

Those were my last thoughts, as my ears rung and I faded into blackness.

Chapter 34

Brianna

"Mu-Muuuuuu! *Boom! Boom! Boom! Boom! Boom!* I'm bussin' at these bitch-ass niggaz! "Where y'all goin', huh! Don't run now! *Lak! Lak-Lak-Lak-Lak!* Hood let the .45's go!

She said, "Bri, get us outta here! I got Mula! The twins were empty, so I grabbed the Four-One off the floor.

"It's on and poppin' now niggaaaaz!" *Booom! Booom! Boooom! Booom! Booom!* Click! .41 on 'E'. Bitch niggaz retreated back into the hallway. A few of'em tryna trap us in. They dumpin'!

Bok-Bok! Bok-Bok-Bok-Bok-Bok!! Lok-Lok-Lok-Lok-Lok! They got me blocked in behind this stove!

"Hood! Hand me the Mac and another clip outta Mula's backpack!" I wanted to tear the shoe box off the front of the gun so these niggaz could feel me comin'! I slapped another clip in his ass! It was time to let Maximum ride! I rose up from behind the stove and opened fire! As I spit, I screamed.

Gggggggg! "Ahhhhhhhhh!" *Gggggg-Ggg-Gggggggggg!* The Mac growled! I hit one of them bitches! Seen'em drop! As we listened, we heard the muffled sounds of the other Mac. I know Maxine. When I heard niggaaz screamin' like hoes, I knew our backup had arrived. For a few seconds, there was nothing but silence. Then, I heard *"Pyt! Pyt*, where y'all at!" I'd know Lue's voice anywhere.

"Lue-Lue! Sweets!" I yelled.

"Yeah, where y'all at, Bri?" Sweets yelled back.

Hood said, "We in here!"

When they came around the corner and saw Hood carrying Mula across her shoulder, Lue dropped to her knees in defeat.

She said,"What-the-fuck happen! Is that—Is she—"

Hood said, "She gon' be a'ight. They dead?"

Sweets said, "Yeah. All of'em touched."

Hood said, "Get up, Lue! Here, take the bags. I got her! Let's go!"

I said, "Hood!"

"What?"

"Her—her mask." My hands were shaking.

"Damn, you right. Throw it on her for me. Stay on point! If it moves, kill it!"

Chapter 35

Gina

I thought today would be another slow one for me. But my God, I was wrong. I got the call a few minutes ago, at approximately 4:43 a.m., while purchasing the usual Cop's breakfast. Red, white and blue. The patriotic colors were flashing from all directions as I pulled up to the scene. The department has everything taped off from 10th in Atkinson, to 10th in Keefe. The looks on the faces of other officers and their body language suggest it's bad. I need to prepare my mind and my body for what I'm about to encounter. So, I took another bite off my chocolate cream-filled Long John, and took a sip of my coffee. It may be the last piece of food I'll see for the next couple hours. And my thick ass do not need to be losing no weight. Wrapping my doughnut up, I put it back in the bag with my other one for later.

I zipped up my quarter-length Wilson leather, and pulled my badge out on its chain, showing off my rank. I've worked damn hard to get here, so I flaunt it proudly. I looked in my visor mirror, checking my hair and makeup before I radioed in. "Damn, you look good," I said to myself, thinking out loud.

"Thirty-two-forty-four. Detective Burke arriving at 1021 Atkinson."

"10-4 Detective. Officers on the scene have reported that we have multiple victims of what appear to be homicide inside the residence. The area has been secured!" the dispatcher responded.

"Copy that." It's still dark out. I jumped out the Crown Vic in my skin-tight jeans and stilettos, coffee in tow as I ducked under the yellow tape. I'm greeted by my friend and commanding officer on the scene.

I took a sip of my coffee, handed it to him, and he handed me his flashlight. I took the lead as he filled me in.

"A'ight, Jamison. What we got?" I questioned.

"We've got ten dead. Eight males, two females. From what I understand, a dope house."

"Another one?" I asked, shaking my head.

"Indeed. It looks to be another case of robbery. The entire fucking scene's a mess. You've got yourself three floors. Bodies from top to bottom. I didn't make it upstairs. Nobody's been in, besides myself and first responders."

He pointed at the house and said, "The front door there is blocked off. You'll have to take the back entrance through the gangway. Thank God it stopped snowing. We've got a lot of prints heading to and from the alleyway. But, who's to say if they belong to the killer, killers or customers?" Trying to stay warm, he blew air into his palms.

I said, "Shit, most likely both. Well, all three. I got it from here. Tell your men to hold the perimeter. Search the alleyways, garbage cans and sewers. Let's see if we'll be lucky enough to find a weapon this time. Wake the neighbors, if they're not already up. Find out who heard, or saw what."

"Canvass, I gotcha. And Burke—"

"Yeah?"

"Watch your step. It's pretty slippery out here, and calamitous in there. Your first presents are on the side of the house."

"Thanks, Jamison."

He said, "No problem, Cup Cakes." I'd like to kick his ass. Talkin' about my butt.

"A'ight, now, watch it!" I smiled. "Get on outta here and go do some work." He nodded and walked away. *Crazy self,* I thought.

I put the flashlight under my arm, then slid the pair of latex gloves on I had in my pocket. Now I'm ready. I spotted two silhouettes on the pavement as I flashed my flashlight and slowly approached the rear entrance. Shining the light on my first victim's face, I recognized Christopher "Packman" Fuller right away. He was a suspected murderer that we could never hold for one reason or another. I'd noticed he's been hit multiple times in the neck and his chest cavity. Several .9mm shell casings were scattered about in the snow. I didn't recognize the woman.

However, I took notice that she'd been shot in the back of the head, twice. She'd died with her eyes open. I take it she'd been executed after Mr. Fuller here, by the positioning of the bodies. Seeing the burn marks on her fingertips tells me she's a smoker. Checking her pockets, I found eighty-five dollars and her ID card. She now had a name.

Sheila. Ms. Sheila Lewis of 1241 Finn Avenue. She was 34 years old. It's a damn shame. I'm not a taker of notes, as you may be aware of by now. Most police officers do that right away. My memory is photographic, which makes me one of the best the department has ever seen. Which was why I don't need no rookie ass partner all up my ass asking a million questions and writing shit down. All that shit comes later. Packman had four-thousand-two-hundred and eighty on him. No ID or nothing. I entered the back door. At first, nothing seemed unusual besides the door standing wide open, and some blood spatter on the steps as well as the walls. But, I knew to expect the unexpected. I'd been outside inspecting for about an hour and a half, so the heat felt good.

As I climbed, there was more and more blood. The first landing was almost completely covered. I've gotta find a way around it in order to enter the apartment without contaminating the scene by stepping in the shit. I noticed a few people already had. There were bloody footprints of different sizes heading outside. Hmm? I don't recall seeing any bloody prints out there, meaning the snow had more than likely covered those possible leads.

Here goes nothing. Stretching my legs as far as I could, I managed to keep my balance as I hopped over the threshold. The lights in the kitchen were still shining bright, so I turned the flashlight off. There was a lot of cocaine left behind. Looking at it, I can easily estimate its street value could fall in the range of forty to fifty thousand. It's right here in plain view. Just sitting on the countertop.

There are four separate hands of playing card, along with four stacks of money on the kitchen table. These dudes were playing Spades when they got bum-rushed. One of 'em had a nice hand too! About seven books! Something tells me that this might be my crew. The same crew I've been after for years. Doing home invasions is their modus vivendi. 'Their way of life.' Sometimes the robberies turned out like this one. Bloodbaths that are deemed catastrophic. Once they start killing, they kill everybody. They've never left a witness. They've always used the same weapons. Nine-milimeters, Shotgun, Thirty-Eights and Forty-Fives. So far, I've found the .9mm shells. They're a smart crew, using new weapons each time they've killed. Although the calibers are the same, our ballistics team can never match the casings to a different crime scene. We've yet to come across any of their weapons, so they must have a pretty sufficient means of disposing of them. I'm counting on them to make a mistake. Just one! All I need is a break. I'm hoping today will be the day 3C will give it to me. I know it's they ass! I'm wondering if it was an inside job. Come to think of it, I caught the twins coming outta here some years back. Did someone let the assailant, or assailants in? Was Ms. Lewis used as a decoy? Or, was she simply at the wrong place at the wrong time? The windows are boarded up. There are casings all over the kitchen floor.

Using my ink pen to get a closer look, I see there are two different calibers here. The bathroom is clean. Nothing.

I approach the first bedroom, following the path the shells have taken me. I see how the casings were ejected from the chamber of the weapon. To the right, and slightly backwards, lies my trail.

My experience tells me they'll lead me to my next victim. I see blood on the doorsill. I made sure not to disrupt the evidence as I pushed the door open further. There he is. He been shot in the back multiple times. Looks as though he was being chased.

"Whatchu was gone do, jump out the window, Eddie?" I asked his soulless body. "It's boarded up, fool!" I shook my head. Eddie 'Ready' Reed. I know some of these dudes from my days on the beat in this area. I know a lot of their mommas too. I didn't even have to see Eddie's face. I know it's him by the unique tat that stretches across his back that reads A.T.K. and "DIME BAG READY", with all the moneybags and dollar signs. Now, somebody had added slugs. I counted the wounds; Eddie had been shot eight times. Seven in his back, and once in his face as he laid on the floor. I closed his eyes, as his mouth hung open. I'm beginning to think maybe—Just maybe all this has something to do with the death of Tersi King. He was also known to the streets as "Atkinson Goldie." He was reported missing by the mother of his child a few months back. The streets assumed he was just off somewhere partying. He was known at times to just pick up and go.

Vegas, Cali, Miami, the list goes on. But two weeks ago, we found his partially decomposed corpse in an abandoned duplex out 32nd Street. He'd been beaten to death. My guess is he was tortured.

The coroner said she'd found teeth and bone in the contents of his stomach. The entire bottom half of his skull in the mouth area had been crushed, and was missing. The M.E. said, finding teeth and bone in his esophagus and stomach suggests to a certainty that he was alive and had actually inhaled and swallowed the dense semi-rigid arthropods of his exoskeleton. The shit made my stomach turn just thinking about it. This is his crew I'm looking at now. Well, at least some of them. Checking Eddie's pockets for clues, I found nothing. His gun, however, was still in his hand. It had recently been fired. Smelling the chamber told me that much. The rest of the rooms were empty as far as bodies were concerned. I gotta make it my business to check with them boys down in the Narc Division and see why this fuckin' dope house was up and running like a grocery store in the first place. Dirty sons of bitches might be in on the take. Oh well, that's IA's business, not mine. I've been down here long enough. Time to make my way back to the back door. I gotta play Ms. Acrobatic Bitch again, and balance myself in these heels through all this damn blood.

Chapter 36

All The Way Up

A lot of it is running down the steps. I see why, now that I'm here. I'm seeing more and more shell casings. While climbing the steps, on the second landing I found four more bodies shot to shit. There's also an automatic shotgun, shotgun shells, and more nine mill casings. There are also some .45 and .380 shells in the mix of things. However, there are more nine millimeter casings than anything else. One of the dudes must have caught a shotgun blast to the head. Half of his shit is blown off. This may be why I don't recognize him. He's gonna need to be ID'd. I do however recognize Tremain Tyler, aka "T-Dog" and Jumar "J-Prince" Jones. Somebody fucked these boys all the way up! They can't be no older than twenty-three, twenty-four. I'd seen all three grow up. Dead already. This crack epidemic is something else. I've been in Homicide for almost five years now, but these last two have been terrible. I checked their bodies for clues. No ID's. I guess we'll have to print our headless man and hope he's in the system. With all their guns laying at their sides, this shotgun seems out of place somehow. This was my crew. I've got no doubt about it. I feel it!

There are no clues. Nothing in the victim's pockets but cash. It looks as if they were caught by surprise, but how? Didn't they hear all the shots? Being shot with a .9mm that was most likely semiautomatic, followed up by a shotgun, left shit real messy. Blood, guts and brains. Medulla oblongata was everywhere. I made it to the top to find two more bodies. I know one to be Andrew "Drew" Judon. I don't know this other one. I checked them both for clues. I again came up with absolutely nothing but cash. Judon is laid out on the landing. The second unidentified subject is stretched out on the attic's steps. I then noticed the apartment's door had multiple holes in it. There's a mixture of shell casings out here. .380, shotgun, more .9mm as well. Throughout the crime scene, I've been seeing these little white balls tickled within the blood here and there. At first, I thought that it came from the stomach, or maybe the brains of my victims, until now. I'd picked a few up and squeezed them. I can't believe it. I—I'll be damned! It—It's Styrofoam! I'm thinking, hmmm, trying to wrap my mind around it as I kneel in front of my victims.

I glanced to my right, peering inside the apartment. I see a set of legs coming from behind the slightly cracked door. This, and all the perforation to the door, tells me the victim was more than likely shot while opening it. Stepping inside, I see Brian "Boomer" Anthony! His chest riddled with bullet holes. I covered my mouth in an attempt to hold back my tears. I'd grown up with his mother. I'd known Brian since he was a baby. I had no idea he was in the streets. I wonder, had *she*— Had she known! His mother! Lord, LaDonna is going to be devastated. She and Angie. She and Brian have always been very close. I kneeled down by his body, took his hand into mine and said a silent prayer. How was Boomer able to hide being this deep in the game from us? Looking around, I see he was responsible for cooking, as well as packaging the product. There was shit everywhere! Enough shit. If the Feds had run up in here, he would've lost his life to prison. Shells were all over the kitchen floor. Bullets have torn through the painted walls, and left holes the size of fifty-cent pieces and quarters behind, as well as in front of me.

Somebody was held up behind this stove. There are a bunch of .9mm shells right here in this area. There's a gun here on the floor that appears to be .41 in caliber. I searched the first bed and bath. Both were empty. The living room was empty as well. The TV is still on. Nintendo game paused. A lot of shells on the floor. Mostly .45's. Jamison said we had two females. There's one more room left I've gotta search towards the front of the apartment. My last victim has to be there.

I walked in the room and turned on the light switch. Wh—what I saw took my breath away. I immediately recognized the clothes I'd bought! Tha—the shoes, her face! "God please! Angie! Angieee! Angie! God, n-o-o-o-o! Not my baaabyyyy!"

It's P.Y.T. til I die!
—**MULA**

Chapter 37

Lue

About ten hours later, we were sitting in Cyn's living room in the apartment she and Money shared. Everybody was all quiet and shit. This morning was crazy as fuck! I took a long, very much needed drag off the big dumb ass Bob Marley joint we had in rotation. Hood broke the tension in the air as I passed her the weed. She took a hit, inhaled and sucked her teeth. She blew out her smoke and looked at Cyn.

She said, "Cyn, you still mad at us, bitch?" and took another pull.

Cyn said, "You damn right I'm still mad atchu ho's! Y'all had no right voting me out because I got a damn daughter! Had I'd been there, that shit would've never happened to Mula! Im'a grown ass woman! I don't need y'all makin' decisions for me and shit!"

Hood said, "You right. We needed you this mornin'. We were just tryin' to look out. It's was in the best interest of our niece. If somethin' were to happen to you, we wouldn't be able to explain it to her. You know?"

"Y'all know how to lie, don'tchu! Right?" Cyn asked, lookin' around the room at all of us.

Hood said, "Of course."

"Well, that's what y'all do! You lie!"

"Damn, that's cold. Just like that?" Hood frowned. She said, "Mu, hit this shit! I know you need it. You gave us quite a scare up there."

"Good thing bro 'nem talked us into investing a couple G'z in them vests, huh?"

"Hell, yeah. If it wasn't for them, my ass wouldn't be here right now." Tears welled up in her eyes as she hit the erb. She'd never come that close to death before. The impact of the .410 caliber slug didn't pierce the vest. But, it hit her so hard it took the air from her lungs, and left her unconscious. It also left a black and blue bruise that'll probably be right there in the middle of her chest for a couple months. My sistah is still in pain.

Hood said, "Cyn, you ain't gotta worry about us voting you out no more, a'ight? Whether you ride with us when the time comes, is totally up to you. And, I mean this goes for all y'all. If—"

Mula stood up and said, "Bitch, don't even go there! These ain't no muthafuckin' tears of fear, or no shit like that! These are tears of anger! Me, not stayin' on point! I wasn't focused, and I got caught slippin'! Me! Of all people!"

Hood said, "Come on, it could've been—"

"Nah, don't get it fucked up though! Unless we all put our feet up and be done with this shit! It's P.Y.T. til' I die! And, y'all right! I fucked up okay! I fucked up! I should've known! Two controllers, the game being set up for two players! It should've told me there was another body! Sh—shit just happened so fast! I just—" Mu broke down. She was bawling. Hood stood up, grabbed her and hugged her. We were all silent.

Hood said, "P.Y.T. Young Mula! I love you." Mu buried her face in Hood's shoulder as she cried. When she looked up again, we were all hugging her.

I said, "We love you too! Like you said, P-Y-T til' we die."

Forcing a smile, Mula said, "Awwww! Group hug!"

As we all smiled through the tears, Sweets yelled, "PYT baby!" We were on some emotional shit.

I said, "I need a drink! Don't y'all wanna drink and smoke some of this fire ass weed we took from them niggaz?"

Drying her tears, Cyn said, "Lue, yo' lil' ass is crazy."

"What? You ain't got nothin' to drink or somethin'?" I asked, drying tears of my own. Everybody burst out laughing.

"Yeah, we got plenty. Money keep this bitch stocked like a wine cellar or some shit. Whatchall want?"

I told her, "Sh-i-i-i-t, Moscato, b-i-i-itch! You got it, bring it! Let's get fu-c-c-cked up!" As soon as Cyn left to get the bottle, I got on Mu ass.

I said, "Mu, slip again! Im'a oooh!" I popped her upside her head and said, "Gotcha, bitch! Ha-haaaa!" I took off runnin'. She tried to catch me, knowing that ass was in no shape to be tryna run. And Mu being Mu, guess what she gon' say as soon as she sat her ass down outta breath?

She said, "Hey, y'all. How-how much money did we get?"

Hood said, "Enough to shut shit down if we decide to get in the dope game. But, nah. Shits too sweet."

"Bri said, "Y'all know what? I'm seriously thinkin' about gettin' a couple of them foe-ones. Them bitches is pow-er-ful!"

"And, oh yeah by the way, Mu! It was a bitch that shotchu. I think it was the nigga Boomer girl or some shit. I know I used to see them around all the time. Anyway, I aired that hoe out for you. You can thank me later with half of your share of that money! What it do?"

We laughed some more, as Mu's face curled up.

She said, "B-i-i-tch, now you know how I feel about my monies! We talkin' about my paper-cheese? Half? Tuh! I think not!"

Cyn came back with a bottle and tray full of drinks.

She said, "A'ight, you thirsty bitches. Come get it."

I said, "See! Now, this what I'm talkin' about! Somebody roll up some more of that shit."

Sweets said, "I'm ordering pizza. We gon' be hungry in a minute."

Hood said, "Shit, call some niggaz. I feel like doin' somethin' tonight."

Rolling her eyes, Cyn said, "Nuh-unn! Not on my phone. They ain't comin' over here! Hood, we can go by yo' crib?"

Flicking her tongue in and out of her mouth, like a snake on steroids, Hood said, "Aw, hell girl. Money ain't comin' home tonight. You might as well getchu some."

"See, whore! Now you done crossed the line!" Cyn smiled, hands on her hips.

It got loud as hell in that living room. Everybody was tryna talk at the same damn time. Some of us agreed with Cyn, and some of us sided with Hood.

Sweets yelled over everybody, "Shhhh! Will y'all be quiet! I'm on the phone with the pizza man!" I think we got even louder, and so did she.

"Yea-Yeah! Let me get a large pepperoni and pineapple, and a large cheese pizza!"

"Yeah! And two liters of Pepsi! Yeah! Yeah, that's it! Ho-hold on! Cyn! Cyyyn!"

"What, Sweets? Damn!"

"What's this address, bitch?" She held up the phone.

"Twenty-two-twenty! North thirty-fifth! Apartment two-twelve!"

"You got that! A'ight! My last name is Sweets! S-W-E-E-T-S! Okay, just ring the buzzer!"

Hood said, "Sweets, hurry up with the phone! My brothers just hit me and put in 9-1-1 twice!"

"Here Hood! I'm done." She handed her the cordless.

Chapter 38

Blood Spilt

While Hood called the twins, we were still laughing, smokin', drinkin' and talkin' shit. As she dialed their number, she said, "This shit ain't over." "They probably need that work. I told them to call me when they were ready." She'd walked into the bathroom. A few seconds later, she came running back out.

"Turn on the TV! Hurry up, y'all ain't gon' believe this shit!" Cyn grabbed the remote and hit the power button. "Turn to channel six!" Hood demanded. When the channel popped in, they were showing pictures of some little girl as she'd aged. First, her infant pictures from the hospital the first day she was born. Then, a picture of her with pigtails, and colorful barrettes. There was a photo from 5th grade, then 8th. Another photo flashed of her and her parents. The last picture they showed was her in a cap and gown. She'd graduated from Vincent. Cyn started reading the commentary exegesis next to her name out loud.

"Nineteen-year-old U-W-M student, Angela Burke, daughter of Milwaukee Homicide Detective Gina L. Burke was shot and killed this morning on—"

"Hold up! I know that ain't the—" Mula interjected.

"Yuuup! That's the bitch that shotchu! Her momma the got-damn po-lice! Look!" Hood pointed at the TV screen. All of our mouths dropped. We were stunned to say the least.

We stood silently in the living room and watched the full press conference.

***

She could barely stand. Blinded by the tears flooding from under blackened sunglasses, her husband held her tightly in his arms. They were asking for information, as they stood at the podium before the bouquet of microphones.

"Hello. My name is Gregory Burke. This morning, our daughter was tragically killed. We're asking for the public's assistance this evening. Any! Anybody—If there's anyone out there with information regarding the person, or persons responsible, please call 1-800-CRIME-STOPPERS. It's toll-free. There will be a five-hundred-thousand-dollar reward for anyone that leads to the apprehension and arrest in this crime. Again, I'm Angie's father. This is her mom, and we need your help."

It took all of her mother's strength, to say what she had to say. Sounded like a threat to me.

She said, "If it takes me to my dying day, I will get justice for my baby." They then stepped away from the microphones and the cameras.

***

Cyn said, "Damn y'all!"

Bri said, "Fuck that bitch! She buss'd first!" She walked over to the table and filled her glass with some more wine.

Hood said, "Well, she was gon' die anyway just being there, so—"

"Y'all right! Fuck'em! This pizza man better hurry the hell up! Fire that other weed up! What y'all waitin' on? Cyn, fuck dat! Turn to Video Soul! I wanna see my bitch, Janet. *Let's Wait Awhile* is my shit! Be-foore we go too faar!"

142

I said, "Cyn, turn to B-E-T! Sweets, please don't sing."
We all laughed.

She said, "Forget-chall! I can blow. Watch! *It's the pleasure principle oho-oho! Oh-aah / It's the principle of pleasure.*" Sweets was singing, doing Janet's signature moves from the Pleasure Principle video.

Hood said, "Cyn, channel thirty-two! Hurry up!" We were dying laughin'.

I said, "Sweets, you-can-not-sing! I think you're tone deaf. Fa-real-fa-real."

She paused. I said, "But you can dance though!"

"I am not! Fuck you, Lue. I ain't off key all the time! Am I, y'all?" She looked around at everybody. There was a moment of silence. Then we all burst out laughing again, as Jody Watley danced across the screen singing about her search for a new love. Sweets' ass was drunk.

Chapter 39

Oletta

I was expecting my sister's arrival. She'd called and said she'd be bringing Dream home any minute. The house was clean, and the laundry was finally done. So, I decided to throw on some chicken. We'd also be having spaghetti and a couple ears of corn for dinner. As I stood in the kitchen over the stove, I was holding the phone to my ear with my shoulder, talking to Saharah.

She said, "Girl, you wouldn't believe what Daz foul ass said yesterday!"

"What he say, girl?" I asked, ready to play Oprah in some shit.

"The nigga come at me like he's a pimp, and I'm one of them lil' hos out there on the track! Like I owe his ass or somethin'!"

"What happened?" I asked.

"The nigga came at me, talkin' about where my money at."

"No, he didn't, Rah!" I instigated.

"Yeah, yes he did!"

"What money he talm-bout! You peeled him?"

She said, "Whaaat? N'aw! He ain't had nothin' to steal. You know I give'em three thousand every time I get my taxes." Saharah hurried into the bathroom and sat on the toilet.

I said, "Em-hmm. What about it?"

"Well, the bank would only let me withdraw twenty-seven-hundred. His sorry ass sweatin' me about the lil' three!"

"I wouldn't give his ungrateful thirsty ass shit!"

I heard the toilet flush. "Saharah, where you at, in the bathroom?"

"Yeah, shoot! I had to pee! I'm done now. I'm washing my hands."

"Ugh! While I'm on the phone!"

"Yup, like you ain't nev—What the hell was that?"

"What?" I asked.

"I heard something. It sounded like something just broke. Hold on." Saharah opened the bathroom door and peered into the living room. Terrified, she quickly stepped back in, closing the door and locking it. "Letta, somebody in my house!" she whispered.

"You got company? Who is it girl? Let me find out!"

"N'aw! Somebody just broke in!"

"Girl, stop playin'." I laughed. "Ain't nobody broke in yo' damn house in the middle of the afternoon."

"Bitch, I'm for-real! I—I just saw somebody in all black with a mask on creepin' through my shit!"

"Rah, where you at?"

"I'm still in the bathroom!" she replied. Backing away from the door, she'd balled up in the corner.

"Get in the shower!" I yelled.

"What!"

"Hide, bitch!"

Careful not to make a sound, she climbed in the shower and closed the curtain.

"He gon' see the phone cord!" her voice shook. Peeping out from behind the shower curtain, she saw the knob on the bedroom door slowly turn.

I heard her yell, "Who is that! Get out my house! I—I'm callin' the po-liiice!" She screamed: "He at the door!"

"Saharahhh! I cried. "Hang up and dial 9-1-1!"

"He at the dooor!" I heard a crash, and Saharah sceaming, "N-o-o-o-o! Get off me! Stop! Lettaaa!"

"Saharahhh! Saharah!" Suddenly the phone went dead. I quickly re-dialed her number, but I got the automated operator. "If you'd like to make a call, please hang up and dial again. If you—" Pressing redial again, I got a busy tone. I dropped the phone and turned off the burners on the stove off. I grabbed a butcher knife, then I ran upstairs and grabbed my car keys. Unaware of the unfolding drama, Lisette walked in with Dream as I rushed back down the steps. My sister immediately recognized the panicky look on my face, and the horror in my eyes.

"Oletta, what's wrong! Whatchu doin' with that knife?" she asked.

"It's Saharah! Somebody just broke in her house! Sett, watch my baby for me."

"Mommmmy!" my two-year-old reached for me. She too had taken notice to the tears in my eyes.

"I'm okay, bay-bee. Stay here with Tee-Tee Sett, okay?" I kissed my baby on her forehead, "Sis, send the police over there! I gotta go!"

"Where she at?" my sister asked, as I rushed out the door.

"She at the house!" I yelled over my shoulder.

"Well, why she—Never mind, just go!" Lisette frantically tracked the phone down. When she found it, she picked it up to call for help. But, she then realized that she didn't know Saharah's address. She'd ran back to the door to try to catch me, but I was long gone.

Chapter 40

High Speeds

Speeding and weaving through traffic, I'd made it to Rah's within minutes. Leaving my car idling in the middle of the street, I jumped out and ran up on the porch. The front door had been kicked in, and the living room was in a disarray.

"Saharah!" I yelled, as I cautiously stepped inside. I got no answer. I rushed to the bathroom, hoping to find my friend taking refuge. But, she wasn't there. Searching further, I found her battered and bleeding from her mouth and nose as she laid unconscious on her kitchen floor with her phone cord wrapped tightly around her neck. Running to her, I gently lifted her head and removed the thin insulated electric cable.

"Saharah, who did this to youuu!" I cried.

"Saharah? Letta!" I heard my sister yell as she entered the home.

"Sett, get my baby outta here! Get us some help! She's hurt! She's hurt b-a-a-a-d! G-o-o-o!" I cried. She ran towards the sound of my voice, gasping as she turned into the kitchen.

"Wha-what happened?" she asked.

"You were supposed to send some help! Where's my baby!" I asked.

"I took her next door to Ms. Milton's! I—I didn't know the address, so I—"

"You—You didn't call!" Shaking her head, by way of saying no, she'd kneeled down beside me.

"Oh my God, Sett! Move! Get out my way!"

"I—I couldn't. I didn't know she—"

I grabbed the phone cord, and plugged it back into the wall. I then connected the receiver and dialed 9-1-1.

"9-1-1, what's your emergency?"

"I need help! I was on the phone with my friend when somebody broke into her house! I'm at the house now! It's blood all over! She—she's on the floor! It was uh—uh, the cord! It was wrapped around her neck! Please hurr-y-y-y!"

"Ma'am, I'm going to need you to calm down so I'll understand you, okay? Take a deep breath. What's your name?"

"O—letta!"

"Oletta, you mentioned a cord being around her neck. Have you removed the ligature?"

"Yeah. it—it was the phone cord."

"Is your friend breathing?"

"I don't kn-o-o-ow! Sett, is she breathing?"

"N'aw! Hell n'aw she ain't breathin! I think she's gone, girl! Is they comin'!"

"She—she said!"

"I heard her. 2427 North 33rd. We've got help in route to your location, but I'm gonna need you to stay on the line. How long ago were you on the phone with your friend?"

"Ab—about ten minutes ago, I guess!"

"Do you know how to do CPR?"

"I—I, no! I've seen it on TV, but—"

"Don't worry, I'll guide you through it. I'm gonna need you to do exactly what I tell you until help arrives. Go to her."

"She's right here!"

"Open her airway by tipping her head back, while lifting her jaw. Look, and listen for breathing."

"Okay, she ain't breathin'!"

"With the head tipped back, pinch her nose closed. Can you do that for me, sweetheart?"

"Yeah, it's done."

"Okay, listen. You're gonna have to set the phone down. I want you to form an airtight seal with your mouth over hers. Give her two slow breaths until her chest rises. Then I want you to follow up with a series of twenty chest compressions, and two more breaths. She needs oxygen, and we need a pulse."

Chapter 41

Timber
A City Broken Into

We'd just had the biggest snow storm our city had seen in a century. Yet and still it was a lot going on. Being nephew was still missing, it was hard seeing Zoi paranoid and suspicious of damn near everybody. She was like a city broken into and left without walls. We could barely have a conversation with her, without her bursting out in tears. Shit, I couldn't blame her. His disappearance has been hard on us all. I thought it to be too cold and too early for trouble. It's freezing, and you'd think people would be indoors trying to stay warm. When Letta called me about Saharah, I felt sick. I'd gotten a little light-headed. Although the roads were hazardous, she came and got me, and we rushed out here to the hospital. After all we've been through in the past few months, I couldn't help but wonder if the individuals that took Eric Junior are somehow responsible for this as well. When we got here, the emergency room was thick! I mean it was packed from wall-to-wall. Saharah's mother, Carla going through it. But hell, we all are. Her husband is doing his best to console her, but nothing could calm her hysteria. She eventually collapsed. They had to take her to the back. They gave her a shot, and a IV for dehydration. She pulled it together. I guess she's okay for the time being. She rejoined us in the waiting area. It seems as though all of Capitol came out to see about my girl.

We're all stressed out. Besides Letta and Sett telling us how they'd found her, and that somebody had broken in her house, didn't nobody know nothing.

All we can do is wait it out, and pray she makes it. J-Dub and his crew came in with Zoi. Every since word hit the streets that Action is still alive; he's been keeping real close tabs on her. Members of his team are now moving like her personal security detail. We thought some bullshit was about to pop off! Saharah's boyfriend, Daz Night and his goons showed up too. Back in the day all these dudes used to be friends. But, now greed and being from three blocks over was reason enough for them not to get along. They've become full blown enemies, and lives have been lost on both sides. They gave each other cold stares, but everybody chillin' out of respect of the situation. Night and Dub made sure it didn't happen, so that's love. The sun fell and the moon came out. Countless hours went by before the doctor finally came out to holler at the Norwoods. He pulled them to the side for an update on Rah's condition. After a brief moment, Mrs. Norwood turned to us. Through the tears, she smiled giving us two thumbs up. It was like a ton of bricks had been lifted off my chest. I could finally breathe. We weren't able to get in there to see her until a few days later though.

***

After peeking through the small window on the door, we slowly stepped inside. My bitch fucked up, but she's alive! Her face is swollen. She has a fractured jaw and two black eyes from a broken nose.

Whoever did this to her had broken her arm, and also two of her ribs. They had shit all up her nose. Seeing our pained expressions, she turned away from us in an attempt to hide her face. Zoi walked over and grabbed her hand.

"Hey babe." She spoke softly.

Letta yelled, "Saharah Gang! We here, girl!" As always, she was just being her loud and animated self. She was still refusing to face us, so I walked around to the other side of the bed and lightly took her other hand into to mine as she laid there with her eyes closed.

"Rah-Rah, look at me. Come, on now!" Acknowledging me, she'd opened her eyes, giving me this hollow stark stare.

She looked up at us, as tears ran down her face. Her eyes loomed toward the front of the bed. Letting go of Zoi's hand, she pointed. We looked. But we were stuck trying to figure out what she was seeing that we didn't. We were so anxious to get up in there to see her, that it had completely slipped our minds that Mrs. Norwood told us that she couldn't talk. That she would be eating through tubes for a while.

"What is it?" I asked. Then it came to me. "The paper and pen? Letta, grab that! Bitch hurry up! She's tryna tell us somethin'!

"Ohhh! Rah, we forgot!" I cried, as Letta handed her the pen and pad. She's a righty, but being her right arm is in a cast she had to use her left hand. Her hands shook uncontrollably as she scribbled her message. When she finished, reading what she'd written left us numb! In a state of disbelief! But, her words were unequivocally clear. *ACTION TRIED 2 KILL ME!*

Chapter 42

Gina

It was like I was having an out-of-body experience. Ever since that day I found my baby dead in the that house, my perspective on things has changed. Disoriented and heavy-hearted, my face feels jowly as tears soak my hollow cheeks. That entire week is grey to me. This sullen morning is no different. Never had I imagined that I'd have to bury my baby. My child. I can barely breathe. Hundreds attended the funeral.

"Let not your heart be troubled; you believe in God; also believe in Me. In My Father's house are many mansions; if it were not so, I would have told you."

Those are the last words I remember.

I could hear the Pastor, but then again I couldn't. All I could see were his lips moving. As they began to lower her in the ground, my body went limp. She was all I lived for. I couldn't let her go. I ran to her, my cold fingers gripping the casket. Screaming her name in anguish, I'd passed out. Thanks to my ex-husband, when I woke up I was back at home tucked in bed. Due to his infidelities, we hadn't been under the same roof in years. Our daughter's death had brought us back together in mourning. I hadn't been out the house in weeks, and he'd been taking care of me. Setting the tray down lightly on the nightstand, he sat on the bed. Reaching over, he ran his fingers though my hair.

"G, you awake? I brought breakfast. Come on. You gotta eat something." He whispered softly in my ear. I opened my eyes.

"Yeah, I'm up. Just laying here thinking, you know." I sat up, resting my back against my oversized pillows. I wrapped my nudity in my comforter. "It smells good. What is it?" I asked.

"French toast, cheese eggs and some bacon. And, as you can see, I also brought you some milk and orange juice." He smiled.

"Damn, where the coffee?" I frowned.

"Oh, the coffee." He cleared his throat, trying to be funny. "I made some. And it's good. I just didn't bring you any. I knew if I did, you wouldn't eat. And—"

"And, I already know. Breakfast is the most important meal of the day. You starting to sound like a broken record around here, ain't you?" I grabbed the platter and removed its lid. Everything looked good and seasoned. Grabbing the fork, I sliced a piece of the toast and forked up some of the eggs. I put the food in my mouth, and mmmm! The syrup, buttery French toast mixed with the eggs were very savory to my taste buds. But, there was something missing. I stuffed a piece of bacon in.

"Emmm! There we go!" I gave him two thumbs up and a nod. After chewing for a few seconds, I swallowed. I said, "See, I'm eatin'. Now can you bring me some coffee, please? You know you be doin' the most. Gon' leave the coffee downstairs." I took another bite, rolling my eyes.

"Okay. But keep eating." He wagged his finger. "You eating a half a meal a day isn't going to cut it."

He got up and left the room. By the time he'd returned, I scoffed down everything he'd brought me. He couldn't believe it. He'd even checked the trash can to see if I'd thrown anything away. The plate was clean. He handed me my coffee and I took a sip.

He said, "That's impossible. You couldn't have eaten all that food that quick." He shook his head.

"Yup. I'm gonna need it for energy." I blew lightly on the steam coming from the cup, and took a gulp of the coffee. I said, "Im'a be going back to work today, so—" tracing the rim of the mug with my index finger. He could tell I was nervous. It's an old habit.

"So, what?" he asked, with a shrug.

"So, I wanna thank you for taking care of me. For last night. For making love to me. I needed that. I ha— hadn't had that in a long time. I've missed you, but—"

"But what? You puttin' me out?" He paced the floor.

"Well, not exactly. It's not like we're back together. We had bereavement sex. You didn't move back in. You were jus— I mean, we were here for one another."

I can't believe this shit! You said you—"

"Look, this isn't goodbye. It's more like, I'll see you later."

"What the fuck? You think you can just use and abuse me when you get ready, huh?"

"Greg, If I'm going to find Angie's killers I gotta focus! I can't allow myself to fall back in love with you. Not right now."

"But, last night you said you love me."

"I was in the moment!" I dropped my head in shame. "Listen, that came out wrong. I do love you. It's just that I'm no longer in love with you. There's a difference. I can't trust you. You understand? Not after all we've been through."

He sighed heavily. "Yeah, I can understand that. But people change, Gina. I've changed. I—"

"Look, not now, okay? Maybe later we'll talk. I just can't do this right now! Sorry I yelled. Listen, I—I'll call you. I gotta go get ready."

Butt ass naked I stood up, let the blanket fall and waltzed pass him, heading for the bathroom. He was still standing there in disbelief when I closed the door. As I turned on the shower, I heard him at the door yelling.

"You gon' do me like that, huh!"

"I'll call you as soon as I get a lead on what happened to my daughter!" I yelled back.

"Our daughter, Gina! *Our* daughter! Did you ever take a second to think about who'll be here for me!"

"You'll be a'ight!"

Believe it or not, I felt his pain. I hated to hurt his feelings, but I had to hit the streets. He'll have to pick up his feelings like I did when I caught his ass cheatin'. Moments later, I felt my entire house quake as he slammed the front door on his way out.

Chapter 43

Morning

The aspect and rate of crimes being committed had the city on high alert from the Mayor to the Chief. Walking in the precinct felt new to me for some reason. Everything seemed surreal. I had to shake it off. As expected, everybody was staring extra hard as I walked towards my desk. I wasn't officially on the clock. First, I'd have to talk to my lieutenant. If I could convince him, he'd talk to the captain. I'd been ordered to take some time off after I'd fainted at the funeral. However, I was also told to come back in when I felt stable. I'll never feel stable again. I didn't need a psych evaluation or no bullshit like that to tell me either. My heart is torn, but I feel like I got my mind right, so here I am.

Jamison hadn't noticed me. He had his back to me sitting at his desk. He was dipping an oversized donut in his coffee when I snuck up behind him.

"Where mines at!" I yelled, startling him. He recognized my voice immediately. Excitedly, he spun around in his chair. I couldn't believe it. He'd even dropped his breakfast on the floor as he stood up to greet me.

"Ha-haaaa! Cakes! Good morning, Detective!" He bear-hugged me, taking me off my feet. "You're back! Ha-haaaa!" He held me tight.

"Morning," I replied. "I can't say it's a good one. But I'm glad to be back. Angie is still depending on me," I said, hugging him back. He put me down.

"From above. From above in Heaven. Let's get a look-at-cha! What's with the shades? I'm gonna need to see those eyes. It's the only way I'll know if you're really back."

"I'm okay. See?" I replied, removing my sunglasses.

"You still look a bit out of it," he replied. "You eat? You want some coffee and donuts? I've got plenty here."

"I'm fine." I waved him off. "Come-on, catch me up. Anything from the guys that caught my daughter's case?"

"Morton and Barnette? Those imbeciles! They're immune to real police work, unlike you and I. See, they don't bleed blue like us, darling." He chuckled, shaking his head. "You're gonna need to take a seat on this. Trust me." I sat my purse down on his desk and pulled up a seat. He sat down, pulling his chair close, so we were face to face and nobody else could hear what was said.

"Nothing, huh?" My shoulders slouched.

"There's nothing to go on according to those two idiots. Being there wasn't a major break in the first forty-eight, they're lost. These assholes are convinced that Angie had some sort of gang ties. And—"

"I don't even wanna hear it! My baby wasn't in no damn gang! They bet not come at me with that bullshit! I'll fuck around and snap!" I spoke through my teeth." We were supposed to be advancing in Tech. I couldn't understand how we hadn't discovered a thing!

"They believe it's a turf war over drugs. I've kept your theory under wraps. You still thinking—"

"I'm knowing, Jamison!" I whispered.

"I know it sucks that you were told to lay off the case. What the hell? Nobody knows there's a connection but us. All they're seeing is a bunch of dead drug dealers. As far as I'm concerned, we're still by the book. If we happen to find Angie's killers in the midst of our investigation of these home invasion homicides—" he threw hands up and shrugged.

"Is McArthur in?" I looked towards his office; he had the blinds closed.

"Yeah, he's in there. Hopefully he's had his coffee. You going in?"

I nodded. "I need my gun and my shield." I sighed.

"Wait a minute. Here, take these with you." He slid me the box of Dunkin' Donuts, but not before removing two.

"Good luck in there, kiddo. As a matter fact, there he is now." He'd stuck his head out the door.

"Burke! What the hell are you doing here! In my office, now!" I grabbed the donuts and rushed over to'em.

"The Charlse case. I think you were on to something," he said as I stepped in and closed the door behind me. He said, "Oh, you brought donuts?" As I handed him the box, he said, "This just came in. Have you heard about this Norwood case?" Opening the box, he grabbed a chocolate covered Long John and bit into it.

"Read about it in the paper. Saharah Norwood off 33rd." I folded my arms in thought.

"Well, you know she's alive, which is a good thing. She's pretty banged up, but she's also talking. Excuse me, writing. Anyway, she says Mr. Charlse is back from the dead."

Chapter 44

Zoo

"Hold—hol-up, y'all niggaz be the fuck quiet! I'm on the phone! Hel-hello. Hey, Aunt Gwen, this Zoo. I mean this, Chris. Yeah, I'm still in the hospital. I'm okay. It's a'ight. I know you had to work. Yeah, the doctor say about another week or two. Yeah, auntie, I know I'm only sixteen. But—I'm not. I'm gon' stay in school, I promise. Ha—have you seen my momma? You ain't talked to her at all to—yeah, I've been callin' home all day. She was supposed to have come back up here this morning, but she never made it. Yeah, but visiting hours over at 9:00, and it's 7:45. Okay, I'll keep tryin', too. Love you. Bye. Fuck ma! Where you at?"

"You gon' call the whole city? Nigga, yo' mufuckin' momma a'ight. Stop worrying so damn much. She probably somewhere with Dexter. Shit nigga, yo' momma look good!"

"Fuck you, Trell! What I tell you about speakin' on her, huh? And who the fuck is Dexter?"

"Big dick Dexter, nigga!" Trell said as everybody laughed. *"You ain't heard? That nigga got dick like a rope!"*

"Whatchu cryin' 'bout?" Tre-Rida asked in a Jamaican accent, mimicking Eddie Murphy's lines from his classic standup show—Raw.

"Fuck y'all niggaz! Y'all mommaz probably with'em! If my leg wasn't broke, y'all know!

U-Tee said, "Aw nigga if yo' leg wasn't broke, what? You ain't gon' do shit." I smiled, but it was just a show for the big *homie. I'm still worried inside. It's not like her. When she say she gon' do somethin' that shit is done. Not hearing from her got me on edge.*

All the homies are up here at the hopital fuckin' wit' me and a couple of the home girls out the hood after we all got shot. I'd thought my girl left, then she walked back in the room.

"Aww bae, I thought you was gone. You bought me some more shit? You so sweet." Dropping the box on the nightstand, she'd let the balloons float to the ceiling.

"What bitch you got sneakin' up here droppin' shit off as soon as you think I'm gone! The bitch probably saw my car out in the parking lot! That's why she didn't come up!"

"What? Whatchu talkin' about?"

"You told me to leave my car and have my momma come pick me up! Tell me why we left! Pulled out the parking lot and erry-thing! Then I realized I left my purse! So we turnt around! I come back in the doors downstairs, and the nurse say some bitch just dropped this shit off at the desk fo' yo' ass! I look at the card on this heavy ass box and it say, 'From Win—Yet with love! Get well soon! Well, let's see what the bitch broughtchu, shall we?" I—I'm knowing what's inside!

"N-o-o-o-o-o! I don't want it! I—I don't want it!" Goodie picked the box up and heaved it into my bed. When it lands, the lid pops off.

I heard the phone ringing coming out of my sleep. I was having a nightmare.

The same one I'd been having for months on in. Glancing over at the clock, it's just a little after 3 AM. That ungodly hour. We'd fallen asleep watching Cujo. Me and Tee are out in Jade Garden at my momma old crib creepin' with some cuties we'd met at the Mall a couple days prior. Robin and Nya were sisters out of Westlawn. Nya was thick, and looked like Blac Chyna. Robin favored the Ruff Riders first lady, Eve. Being it's the only way I can hear her voice again, as always I let the phone ring and let the machine pick it up. I've listened to her message thousands of times. And will listen a thousand times again. I won't rest until I avenge her death.

I'mmm ev-erry wo-man/It's all in meeeee/Anythang you want done baby/I'll do it naturallly/

My mother sang along with her favorite singer of this world before she greeted us. "Hey, y'all, this Chaka. I'm sorry I can't come to the phone right now. If you'd be so kind as to leave a message, I promise I'll get back to you as soon as possible. So, after the beep you know what to do. God bless!" I thought it might of been Goodie ass callin' out here lookin' for me. She knew I came out here occasionally to breathe and vibe off the connection to my momma. To my surprise, it wasn't. I heard a raspy voice calling out to me as I listened.

"Zoo! Zoo-ooh! Pick up the phone. A mu-fucka need to-holla-atchu boyyy."

Maneuvering my body as I laid behind Nya on the couch, I reached over my head and grabbed the phone.

"Who dis?" I whispered into the phone.

"Th—this who? How the fuck you get this number?" I sat up and climbed over Nya, tryin' not to wake her. She stirred a little bit. "Oh, where she at? She came through there lookin' for me? Ho—how long ago? Nah, where the fuck you niggaz been at? Niggaz ain't seen you and Ross in a minute. Fuck them other niggaz. My lil' nigga? Yeah, I got the message. Y'all was being funny. That was a joke, right." I smiled. These niggaz was always playin'. "Whaaat? You serious!" I couldn't believe my ears. I'm looking at the phone in disbelief. "That was y'all that smoked Chewy nem! Aw—aww, that's yo' word huh! I gotcha word? You—y'all want what! On-my-momma, nigga, listen to you! Nah, you listen, big homie! Check it out, 'cause I'm serious too! I ain't given you bitches shit! 24th through 42nd me, nigga!" Snatching the line out the wall, I threw the base and the receiver across the room. I regretted it soon as I'd done it. What could I gain by tearin' up my momma shit?

"I can't believe these niggaz got the nerve to make demands!" I yelled in frustration.

"Whoa! Who was that? The Twins?" U-Tee asked groggily, raising up from the pallet he and Robin made on the floor in front of the TV.

"Nah, Po bitch-ass!"

"What he say?" he asked.

"Man, fuck them niggaz!" I spat.

"What he say, Zoo!" he asked again.

"Dog, the shit ain't worth repeating, 'cause it ain't happenin!" The ladies just stared as I paced back and forth in my boxers. Flopping down in the leather over seat, I held my head. My shit was starting to throb.

Tee said, "Look, my nigga. I'm with you through whatever! But you need—" he shook his head. "I need to know everything. You hear me? You can't have me out here blind! What up?" I didn't reply. I thought being at my momz apartment would bring me comfort. But I felt like I was losing my mind thinking about all the game has taken from me. Yet, niggaz wanted more. Though my uncle got what he deserved, things haven't gone as planned. Though Congo and Spree remain loyal, other old heads from the hood have rose against me. I would've never thought Po and Ross would be among those who'd cross me. Now I knew they were behind it all from the beginning. Though me, Blue, and Famo got popped and survived, I'm knowing there's no mercy in these streets. In a war with 3C, I'd lost my mother, Brando, Geom, Class, Trell, Rida, Fly and more. They're all like seeds in my head, screamin' that retribution of payback and pain.

"Zoo!" U-Tee nudged me. "What that nigga say?" he asked.

I looked up at him. "He said they behind that Zulu shit. They want fifty bricks and half the territory. He say if I give it to'em, I got his word there will be no more blood spilt."

"So, you sayin' Odds and Chewy—"

I nodded.

"Oh yeah? Robin, y'all get dressed so we can get y'all up outta here." Walking towards the bathroom, he looked back and said, "You know what time it is, don'tchu? Be king, my nigga."

Chapter 45

Action

As a specter in the night, I'd watched them from the shadows. I'd been surveying the operation for weeks. From the looks of things, niggaz hadn't missed a beat since Rock's death, or my spurious demise. I'm pleased to see how they've been handling the money. To me, it's affirmation that I'd taught my souljaz well. I'd groomed them to be Generals, and in turn Dookie had become just that. He'd taken over. All the spots were still up and running as if I'd never left. Duckin' the law was easy when nobody was looking, but now I'd been exposed. No longer was it merely rumored that I'm amongst the living. My mugshot is being plastered primetime on every news outlet for miles. I was now included in the statewide manhunt, said to have the potential to stretch nationally. Two thousand federal and local authorities have joined forces in search of Weight after his pernicious escape. They're also on the lookout for the killers of Angie Burke. Crazy muthafuckaz even say I'm a suspect in the kidnapping of my own son. I made the front page of the Journal Sentinel.

How Saharah managed to survive the punishment I'd put on her mystified me. I'd underestimated her will to live. I hadn't expected her to put up the fight she had. When I left, I'd thought surely she'd taken her last breath. At the stash house, I opened the safe mounted to the floor in the basement. The cash I'd put away for a rainy day was still neatly stacked inside. I stuffed it inside my duffel bag and zipped it up. I also grabbed the two twin Sigs off the shelf.

Hearing something behind me, I swung around with both guns up, ready to open fire.

"Whoa! Aye, it's just me! It—it's just me, my nigga! I told you I was comin'! What up!"

"You're late! You was supposed to been here fifteen minutes ago. Did you make sure you weren't followed?"

Dookie scoffed as he stood frozen at the bottom of the basement's stairs with his hands up.

He said, "Yeah, nigga, damn! I walked, and circled the block like you told me! Whatchu on! Stop playin' with them muthafuckin' gunz!" Lowering my weapons, I smiled.

"What up, boy?" I tucked the heat. Dropping the bag, I walked over to my homeboy. "What up?"

"Man, my nigga! Good to see you! Niggaz thought you was dead!" he replied as we shook up and embraced. "What happened?" he asked. "You all over the TV and shit! What's this shit with Saharah? I know you—"

"Not here. We gotta move. Come on. I'll tell you about it in the car. Dookie followed my lead as we headed outside and hopped in the heavily tinted black Nissan Maxima. Unbeknownst to either of us, we were being watched.

***

Doe

Yo, after we handle these niggaz, what we gon' do with this damn baby? Telesis gettin' too attached to his lil' ass as it is. I keep having to remind her silly butt that he ain't none of her child." I said, peering out the back window, staring at the house we'd watched Action and Dookie creep in.

Teague said, "Well, if we keep'em, we gotta feed'em and keep'em hid."

"Man, that little nigga and ya manz hotter than a bitch. If we kill his little cryin' ass, then what?" Moo asked, looking over at Teague riding shotgun.

"You already know. Then we'd have to get rid of the body. But we ain't gon' do that. It's Christmas. He's a kid. He's innocent in this. Just relax. Give me some time to think on it. I'll take care of it!" Teague replied.

"They pullin' out now!" I yelled.

Action

As the bass and the euphonious horns of *Move the Crowd* condensed and Rakim began his rhythmical flow, I backed out the driveway. Me and Dookie both bobbing our heads as Rakim pressed inferior poets, we were in traffic. Bemused at heart, Dookie had a question.

"So, what up, 'A'?" he asked. "I was your everyday nigga. Why you ain't been got in touch with me?" I glanced over at him.

"I'm out for blood, Dook. I didn't wanna get you involved in this shit. Them bitches tried to kill me. And now they got my son."

"Wh—who you talkin about? You know who got Lil' Eric!"

"You remember the bitch Bri and her buddies?"

"Hell yeah. How can I forget! We met them at the rink. They fine as—"

"Listen, fuck all that! That's who shot me! And that's who snatched Junior!"

"What?" he frowned in disbelief. Bending forward to turn the music down, he wanted to be sure he was hearing me correctly.

I said, "Yeah, my nigga. That's who ran up in my shit and got us for all that paper." I could tell reflective memories were shooting through his mind.

"Wait a mutha-fuckin' minute. You tellin' me—"

"That was them in the Gremlin masks, nigga! Have I ever bullshitted you! Huh?" Taking it all in, there was a moment of silence as he tried to process what he was hearing.

"And Saharah?" he asked, as we passed familiar landmarks back in the inner city. We'd known her our entire lives. He knew she had no part in all this shit. At least that's what he hoped. I exhaled, turning my head as I bent a lefthand turn. I couldn't even look at my roadie. I felt guilty. I knew it ran deeper for him. He'd always had a crush on Saharah.

I said, "Shit got out of hand. I went through there. I just wanted to scare her. It wasn't supposed to go that far. I—I just needed some answers. You know Zoi fuckin' with the nigga J-Dub?" I glanced over at'em, but quickly turned my head back towards the road.

"Yeah, I've seen'em. I've also seen what you did to Saharah. Damn, nigga."

As I reclined in the leather, we came to a stop on Sherman and North Avenue. As we sat at the red light, a grey truck pulled beside us. In my peripheral, I caught a glimpse of the chrome and the scintillation from the barrels.

As I ducked, I hit the gas, yelling, "Dook, get down, niggaaaah!" The tires spun in place on the dirty ice before snagging enough traction to bolt forward. A barrage of bullets was sent into the passenger side, swiss-cheesing the door, shattering the windows, sending the freezing temperature gushing inside. Due to oncoming traffic traveling north and southbound up the Boulevard, we had a hard time making it through the intersection. A hail of bullets also shattered the back window, sending shards of glass bursting towards the front of the car. Rounds echoed like diabolic curses from hell as my pursuers gave chase. I glanced back as I made a right on 44th. I was relieved to see the truck had kept straight heading up North Avenue as sirens sounded in the distance.

I'm the intelligent, wise on the mic / Right in front of your eyes 'cause I am a surprise—Rakim sang, my adrenaline was pumpin'!

"Dook! Dook, ge—get up! You hit! I see blood, nigga, you hit!"

My nigga was folded foward with his head between his legs beneath the dash. I grabbed him by the back of his Peacoat, pulling him back into the seat. His eyes were wide open, but he was gone. He'd been hit several times. Lookin' in my rearview, I spotted the police closing in behind me. I had no choice to try to bail before backup arrives and I'm completely surrounded. Pushing the pedal to the floor, I blew the stop sign on Meinecke. I gotta put as much distance as I can between us, if I'm gonna have any chance of gettin' away on feet.

Dipping in an alley between 45th and 46th, I grabbed the money and got up out that bitch. However, making it to my destination on Clark where SoVee awaited me is going to be difficult. I realized I was hit too! The squad cars racing up the alley behind me left me with few options.

***

Doe

Meanwhile, a few blocks over in a Walgreen's parking lot, Weight wiped the truck down. He then jogged across the street to hop in the car with us.

"Get in, nigga! Hurry the fuck up!" I yelled.

"I—I'm in! Gemme that! Hit the block! Hit the block, Moo!" Weight demanded, reachin' for the AR-15 in the back with me, resting across my lap. Moo slowly pulled from the curb. I started to hand it to him too. But Teague shook his head.

He said, "The police thick out here. Moo gon' get us up outta here."

Chapter 46

Gina

When I heard we had Eric Charlse in custody, I couldn't wait to sink my fangs into'em. He'd been booked on a series of charges, including kidnapping, possession of a firearm by a felon, fleeing and eluding, first-degree murder of one, and attempted first-degree murder of three other police officers. He'd also been charged in the home invasion and attempted murder of Saharah Norwood. He'd been shot, but the wait is over. He's been patched up, and officially released into our custody as of 9:00 o'clock this morning. That ass is mine. I'd set the scene in the interrogation room to my liking. The two Sig Sauers he'd used were sitting just outside his reach. I wanted him to see'em. His prints are all over them, so I'm hoping for a confession on most of the charges. His file was on the table as well, displaying pictures of his victims. I want his ass to sweat. After an hour and 45 minutes of letting everything sink in, I'm ready.

When I walked in, he was seated in a chair, handcuffed to the wall. He was slouched over. At first, he appeared drained. But then he sat straight up. I sat my coffee down, and took a seat directly across from him. Before I introduced myself, I crossed my legs, giving him enough thigh to remember until he dies. I pressed *record* on the tape recorder to my left.

"Hello, Mr. Charlse. I'm Burke. I'm a homicide detective. Have you been read your rights?" He nodded. "I'm sorry, but I'm gonna need a yes or no answer, please.

"Yeah," he replied.

"How are you today? You look pretty damn good to be a dead man. I mean—if I must say so myself." He didn't say anything. He just looked at me, sneered and dropped his head. "I've got a few questions for you. If you don't mind. But, before we start in on the bad, and it's a lot, how about we start with the good stuff. Your son?" He looked up at me. "Whoever had him returned him safely yesterday. He wasn't harmed. He was checked out, and he's healthy. No malnutrition or anything. He was well taken care of."

Again, he didn't say a word. He turned up his nose, like I stunk or somethin'.

"Damn, okay! Just wanted you to know. Zoi's happy. For some reason, I thought you would be too. That's if yo' ass ain't have nothin' to do with it."

"Spss!" he scoffed. He said, "Y'all dumb asses would think I had somethin' to do with that, huh?"

"Didju?" I rolled my eyes. "Hm! Strange enough, soon as yo' ass is in custody, somebody miraculously rings the door bell and vanished, leaving him on the front porch. You know a little about disappearing, don'tchu?" Giving me the silent treatment again, he just stared.

I said, "Well, do you know anybody that goes by the name, 'Esis? That's who he's referring to as his second mommy." He shook his head.

"You don't, huh? Boy, you're one lucky son-of-a-b-i-i-i-i-tch! Take a look at that car you jumped out of." I slid the photos of the shot up Maxima in front of him. And, with his friend still inside how he'd left him. "Do you have any idea on who tried to kill you?" He made eye contact.

"Again, I'm sorry. I meant *kill you again*. I was at your house. I worked your murder for a second. Was it the same person or persons that tried to kill you the first time?" He was still silent. "Would you like to start from the beginning and tell me who caused those wounds to your face and head? I would also like to know who helped you fake your death." I've got his attention. I can tell how he's looking at me.

He said, "You know, sometimes we revisit the past in order to write our futures?"

"What is that? Some Shakespeare? What's with the riddle? Boy, stop playin'." I shrugged and smiled.

"You ain't never heard that saying before?" he asked, as I took a sip off my coffee. I shook my head.

"Mm-mmm!" I swallowed. "Why? Should I know it for some reason, Mr. Charlse?'

"You should." He smiled.

I said, "Look, lemme keep it real with you. You're in a lot of trouble here! You killed a cop, and wounded a few others! We don't have time for games. These guns are yours! Ballistics confirmed they were used in the crimes you've committed! We've got witnesses! Plus, we gotcha prints! I'm sure you're aware by now that your wife's friend identified you as her attacker! You entered her domicile and—"

"Your daughter got killed, huh?" he cut me off.

"What!" Now, he has my attention. And full! Pausing, I looked at him with a flummoxed expression on my face.

"I said, your daugh-ter!" he spoke slowly. "She's dead, right?" Trying to keep it together, I closed my eyes in thought.

He said, "What's wrong? No smiles? Y—you think you can come in here and talk about my family! We can't speak on yours?" He cocked his head to the side.

Lacing my fingers together, I grabbed my knees as my legs began to rock back and forth. Clearing my throat, I could feel my body starting to perspire.

"Mr. Charlse, do you know anything about my daughter's murder?" I asked, as calmly as I could.

"Good question." He chuckled. "I might." He looked me in my eyes.

"What the fuck you mean, you might?" I stood up over him. He looked up at me like I'm crazy. I was! I am! He doesn't know me!

Grinning, he said, "Like I said! I—might." He sat back in his chair.

"I know it ain't have shit to do with no bullshit turf war. The shit they'll put in the newspaper. Em-em-emm! Damn, she was a beautiful somethin' too." He'd struck a nerve only the heart and God knew. I rushed him. Grabbing him by the neck, ramming his head into the wall.

"Whatchu know!–What do you knowww! Tell me got-dammiiit! You tell me nowww!"

As I was choking his ass and bangin' his head against the wall, the taps on the two-way glass turned into pounds, but I ignored them. I'd zoned out. Before I knew it, Jamison was pulling me off him, and ushering me out the room as I kicked and screamed, "Whatcu kn-o-o-o-o-w!" Jamison slammed the interrogation room's door, cutting into my rage. McArthur, my lieutenant awaited me on the other side of the door, accompanied by FBI Agent Gragh. I hadn't even noticed that I was in tears.

"Burke, what the hell! What are you doing in there!" McArthur yelled. "You know better! You can't assault the guy simply because he says something about Angela! That's not how we work here, and you know it! What's wrong with you!" he scolded.

"Lieutenant, I'm sorry. I—I just! I lost it for a second! Give me another shot, I swear—"

"I don't know!" he shook his head, wearing a look of disappointment in his eyes. He said, "You're a mess!"

"N'aw, I'm okay. See?" I dried my eyes. "I'm close! Plea-e-e-e-z-e!" I begged.

He said, "Okay! Get back in there. But I swear, if you so much as to lay a finger on him, I'll have your badge! Do we understand each other?" I nodded in agreement. "Get her some Kleenex for God's sake!" he nodded at Jamison. He and Gragh stepped back in the observation room. I got my shit together after a few minutes, then stepped back in.

"Mr. Charlse, forgive me for my actions." I apologized immediately and took a seat. "Look, I've got a big problem." I looked into his eyes.

"I know." He rubbed his head. "You lookin' for your daughter's killers. It's driving you nuts, huh?" he laughed.

"I—I need some names. You got some?"

"Look no further than the mirror. They're just like you." He sneered.

"Wha—whatchu sayin'? You saying the police killed my baby?" I smacked my lips. "Boyyy! You so full of shit your eyes brown. You don't know nothin'." I waved him off.

"Did I say pigs?"

"Whatchu tryna say?"

"Bitch, you figure it out. I ain't tellin' yo' ass nothin' else! I wanna deal. Get my lawyer in here." Just like that, the interrogation is over. I heard a light tap on the window.

"Well, you've asked for a lawyer, so we're done. For now, I can't promise you a deal, but I'll see what I can do. I leaned in. We were nose to nose. "You know somethin'? Don't play with me!" The door flew open.

"Burke!" I heard McArthur's booming voice. I looked up to see him standing in the doorway with a white guy carrying a briefcase.

"His lawyer." McArthur nodded for me to step out the room. I gathered the evidence. As I got up, I was mean mugging his ass the entire time.

On my way out, he yelled, "You wanna know who murdered that lil' bitch! Get me a deal!" He was trying to push my buttons. And, he had. *I gotcho lil bitch*, I thought to myself. I went to my desk and dialed a number that I hadn't in a long time. She answered. The last time we'd seen each other was at a funeral. There were no words to be spoken. We just gave each other the nod. I see you.

"Buttercup? Hey, it's me, GB. I—I know, right? Long time. I—I needju. Meet me where we used to play as kids. Tonight, same as always, a'ight? See you there."

Chapter 47

Cuppy
—Love Me a Gangsta.

After momma died, I'd chose one path and she'd chosen another. I hadn't heard from her in years. So, to actually hear her voice brought me to tears. I can't believe my niece is gone! I'd seen the news conference, and it killed me inside that I couldn't be there with her. I've pretty much been a loner these days, trying to run from the pain. I spend most of my time traveling the world, resting in different havens. You can say, I've been fucked up for a while. This will add another year to those I'll hate to remember. A while back, they found my husband's head mounted on a pole on 24th in Burleigh in place of its stop sign. Somebody had carved the word 'GREED' into his forehead. His torso was found some blocks up, on 40th. The rest of his limbs were scattered throughout the hood. From that first day we met, he took care of me. I guess I somewhat took to him like my father, being ours was never around. He was older, but age ain't nothin' but a number to me.

Though Gina ain't like him for me, I love me a gangsta. And, he loved me. She was always busy with school, work, and stuff. She'd vowed she'd do any and everything in her power to separate us. She'd even asked me to choose between him and the family. Me choosing him changed everything. It tore us apart. She knew he sold drugs, and that went against everything she's ever stood for. It broke my heart when she told me, as long as I was with him, that she never wanted to see nor speak to me again.

She harassed him every chance she got. She'd pull him over, search his car without consent or probable cause. Complaints to her superiors went unanswered. Her word against his. She hated his guts! But in all that, she'd heard about his death, and she and Angie joined us in his inhumation. She didn't say a word. The look in her eyes told me she loves me beyond our internal wars. I wanted badly to go to her at Angie's funeral, but I feared rejection. Besides, I didn't know what to say. I should have! She'd always reminded me how deep love ran when we were younger. I should've just told her I love her, if nothing else. She'd shown me love in times I knew I didn't deserve it. When momma passed, I got wild and disobedient. Ever since we were babies, Gina believed her mission from Yahweh was to save our community. I never really thought she would actually become a police officer. With all the evil that went on around us! It just didn't happen where we're from. In the end, good prevailed. She did it! I've never gotten the chance to tell her I'm proud. My big Sis, out here fighting crime and shit. Me, on the other hand. I've done many things to survive. See, unlike your typical 'hustler's wife,' I didn't just sit back looking cute and collect the money to go spend. I'm assuming you know! Behind every powerful black man there's a strong black woman. At times we're in front. I'm that bitch! Me and my king were partners, so I was hands on in everything.

From vettin' niggaz, moving the product through the pipeline, to eliminating threats. The streets know how I get down. However, apparently, a lil' nigga that worked for us, callin' himself French, hadn't heard. To refreshing everybody memory, I had to make an example out his ass. I needed the soldiers to know not to fuck with me when it came to my paper! He'd been movin' keys for us for a minute, and we were paying him well. But, no matter how much you looked out, to some it's never enough. It started off slow. He'd come short a G' here, another G' there. Then he graduated to threes, fours, eights and even nines. Little did this bitch-ass nigga know, I don't forget nothin'! I count everything. Stupid nigga! I played it cool. He could've stayed out of sight of the barrel, but I'd made up my mind. The next time pussy-boy came up shy of a penny, I was killin' his ass! Aw, he thought shit was super-dupper sweet. The next drop, he showed up short ten thousand. That raised his total debt to 30k! We were having a team gathering. I always cooked for our favored, and he'd become one of my husband's for some reason. I didn't like his pretty ass. He was right on time for dinner out at the mansion. I'd shown him in, and into the TV room where all the men were watching the NBA Playoffs, waiting for the food to get done. I'd taken the money he'd given me up to our room, counted it and put it with the rest of the money we'd received that day. Tired of his excuses, he was beyond redemption. I was tired of this fool comin' in here smiling, giving me what he thought we should have.

I got ready and headed down to tell the men that they could start washing their hands and taking seats in the dining room as I always did. Once everybody was seated, I came out with the curry chicken, fish, spaghetti, salad and the other dishes I'd prepared, setting them on the table. Everything was set. I said a prayer, and told them to dig in while I checked on their dessert. I waited about ten to fifteen minutes, then grabbed a butcher knife. Hiding it behind my back, I walked into the dining room. Sorry to spoil their appetites, but I had to appease myself.

"Y'all gettin' full?" I asked. My baby looked up at me and nodded with a smile. All I heard was smackin', "Emm-hm!" and the clatter of the silverware from the others. Walking up behind French, I swung, plunging the knife into his stomach from the side. Reacting, everybody jumped up, including French, trying to grab me by my throat.

J.L. yelled, "Nigga, get your hands off my wife! Cuppy, what the hell!" as I gritted my teeth, twisting the knife. I looked French directly in his eyes as I pushed him back into his seat. "I know you getting real full, nigga!" I barked, as he gasped for air. I walked over and snatched my husband's gun off the table and put one in his chest. He tried to grab me, but I brushed him off.

"Cu—Cuppy, what the hell is you doin'! What's wrong with you!" J.L. asked. Everybody else had their hands up.

"Cuppy—what! Why you—"

"That muthafucka was short, again! He was on time to eat though, huh!"

He said, "Everybody just go! Get out. I'll call y'all later. Cuppy, you done got blood everywhere and fucked up the food!"

"It's some more in the kitchen," I replied, folding my arms as the team filed out.

"A'ight, y'all. Let me take care of this."

"You need any help?" Congo asked, looking at the body as he was last to leave.

"Nah, I got it. I hope my neighbors ain't hear that shot," J.L. replied as he walked him out.

Everybody left. I didn't have to worry about them talkin' to the police. I had muthafuckaz believing me and Sis were on the best of terms. That if a statement ever popped up, they'd be dealt with accordingly. It was far from the truth. But that small lie had me feeling untouchable. I'd been getting away with murder for years. I knew word would spread not to play with the deniro, and that was the whole point. J.L. was lettin' the nigga steal and get away with it. Fuck all the money he'd made for us. He was takin' his cut, plus a percentage of ours! Somehow, in the process of dumping the body that night, recognizing J.L.'s car, Gina pulled it over. Though he was always clean when she sweated him, today was different. This time, her search for dope resulted in her finding a body in the trunk, and me behind tint in the driver seat. She thought I was making a run for him. After discovering the body in the trunk, she walked back to my window. I dropped my head.

She said, "You still with that nigga, huh? I thought I told yo' lil' ass I never wanted to see you again." She shook her head, went and got back in her cruiser and left. She'd let me go.

Chapter 48

Holdja Head

Excited to see her, I was already at the cemetery dressed in black when she pulled up. When we were younger, other kids were spooked of this place. But we saw it as a playground we could have all to ourselves at night. I was standing at the resting place of our mother and my sister's daughter. She got out, and I ran to her. Wew! We cried and cried! I hugged her until it hurt.

"Where your car at? Girrl, how you get here?" she asked.

"I walked. I had a lot on my mind. I've been here for a while, just talkin' to Any and Ma!" I replied.

"Okayyy!" she waved. "I was out here yesterday. Thinking about old times."

"Gina, I'm so sorrrry!"

She said, "Come-mo now. No time for regrets, Buttercup. You know what momma used'ta say ... *you gotta holdja head*!" She smiled. "Besides, I wanna show you somethin.' Look." She walked back to her car and popped the trunk. Looking in, I said, "What the fuck is this!" As soon as he saw me his eyes got big.

"Aw, this Lowly off Cap—"

"I know who he is!" I whispered. "And he knows me! What the hell is he doin' in yo' trunk!"

"I'll explain on the way. Come on. Help me get'em out." Strange as it may sound, I was nervous! She was calm as fuck! I mean, damn. We're from two different worlds. Though she's my sister, I still saw her as the law.

I hadn't done any crimes in midst of somebody wearing a badge before. I felt like I was being set up or some shit for a minute.

"Hold on! Ho—how? Where you get this nigga from?" I asked.

"I pulled his punk-ass over. How you think?"

"But you—"

"Uh-unn! No questions, Cup! You owe me that much. You from the streets. You know how it go. This whatchu do, ain't it?" My mouth dropped. She said, "What? You surprised? Yeah, I know. Now freeze all the questions and let's get to it."

She's right. I owe her big time. We pulled him out. She up'ed a chrome.380 with a compressor screwed on its barrel as we walked him towards the other side of the graveyard.

She said, "I think he may know something about Angie's murder, but he actin' stupid."

"What makes you think that?"

"The liberty in speaking to a dead man this morning led me in his direction," she replied.

"What? A dead man?"

"Their old leader, Mr. Eric Charlse. You may know him as Action."

"Yeah, I know that fool."

"Well, he was acting like he knew somethin' about my baby's death, but he wants a deal. There's no way the D.A.'s office is gonna offer up. He murdered a cop. So, I'ma snatch these little muthafuckaz up one by one! I don't care if I gotta burn every last one of'em. Somebody gon' tell me what I wanna know."

She told him, "You've got five seconds once that tape come off!"

"But, what makes you think he knows somethin'?" I asked.

"Lowly here run shit. Now that his man Dookie is dead. Ain't that right, Lowly? The homies say you callin' shit now."

We'd stopped in front of a hole that was freshly dug. Seeing the casket had me trippin'! She'd dug a muthafucka up! I turned to her. The blackness in her eyes was something I'd never seen in her.

"Gina, whose grave is this? Wh—who you done dug up?" If Lowly wasn't scared, I was scared for'em.

"Oh, that's Dookie. He ain't gon' mind a lil' company. Whatchu think, Low? You think Dookie a mind you stayin' with him for a while?" She snatched the duct tape from his lips and shoved him in the hole with his hands bound behind him. "One!" she began her count.

"Wait—wait—wait!" he begged, as he rolled over onto his back on top of the casket.

"Two!"

"Cuppy, pleeease! Talk to her! Th—this bitch crazy! I swear I—"

"Three! Talk, nigga! Who killed my baby? Butter can't help you!" She raised the gun, pointing it at his head. "Four!"

"You—you can't kill me! You th—the po-lice!" She pulled out a paper bag and held it to the chamber of the gun to catch the shells.

"Em-mmm! That's where you wrong. First, I'm a mother. Time's up." She pulled the trigger six times. She then looked at me and said, "Come on. Help me bury this bitch. But, first thing first, here." She reached into her pocket. Pulling something out, she extended her hand to me closed fist.

She said, "I believe this belongs to you." She handed me my cross. "Now hurry up. I wanna go talk to momma and Angie before we leave. And I'm thinking: *Daaaamn! I thought I was the gangsta in the family.*

—To be continued

Lock Down Publications and Ca$h Presents
Assisted Publishing Packages

BASIC PACKAGE	UPGRADED PACKAGE
$499	$800
Editing	Typing
Cover Design	Editing
Formatting	Cover Design
	Formatting
ADVANCE PACKAGE	**LDP SUPREME PACKAGE**
$1,200	$1,500
Typing	Typing
Editing	Editing
Cover Design	Cover Design
Formatting	Formatting
Copyright registration	Copyright registration
Proofreading	Proofreading
Upload book to Amazon	Set up Amazon account
	Upload book to Amazon
	Advertise on LDP, Amazon and Facebook Page

***Other services available upon request.
Additional charges may apply

Lock Down Publications
P.O. Box 944
Stockbridge, GA 30281-9998
Phone: 470 303-9761

Submission Guideline

Submit the first three chapters of your completed manuscript to ldpsubmissions@gmail.com. In the subject line add **Your Book's Title**. The manuscript must be in a Word Doc file and sent as an attachment. Document should be in Times New Roman, double spaced, and in size 12 font. Also, provide your synopsis and full contact information. If sending multiple submissions, they must each be in a separate email.

Have a story but no way to send it electronically? You can still submit to LDP/Ca$h Presents. Send in the first three chapters, written or typed, of your completed manuscript to:

LDP: Submissions Dept
P.O. Box 944
Stockbridge, GA 30281-9998

DO NOT send original manuscript. Must be a duplicate. Provide your synopsis and a cover letter containing your full contact information.

Thanks for considering LDP and Ca$h Presents.

NEW RELEASES

BLOODLINE OF A SAVAGE 1&2
THESE VICIOUS STREETS 1&2
RELENTLESS GOON
RELENTLESS GOON 2
BY PRINCE A. TAUHID

THE BUTTERFLY MAFIA 1-3
BY FUMIYA PAYNE

A THUG'S STREET PRINCESS 1&2
BY MEESHA

CITY OF SMOKE 2
BY MOLOTTI

STEPPERS 1,2&3
THE REAL BADDIES OF CHI-RAQ
BY KING RIO

THE LANE 1&2
BY KEN-KEN SPENCE

THUG OF SPADES 1&2
LOVE IN THE TRENCHES 2
CORNER BOYS
BY COREY ROBINSON

TIL DEATH 3
BY ARYANNA

THE BIRTH OF A GANGSTER 4
BY DELMONT PLAYER

PRODUCT OF THE STREETS 1&2
BY DEMOND "MONEY" ANDERSON

NO TIME FOR ERROR
BY KEESE

MONEY HUNGRY DEMONS
BY TRANAY ADAMS

Coming Soon from Lock Down Publications/Ca$h Presents

IF YOU CROSS ME ONCE 6
ANGEL V
By Anthony Fields

IMMA DIE BOUT MINE 5
By Aryanna

A THUGS STREET PRINCESS 3
By Meesha

PRODUCT OF THE STREETS 3
By Demond Money Anderson

CORNER BOYS 2
By Corey Robinson

THE MURDER QUEENS 6&7
By Michael Gallon

CITY OF SMOKE 3
By Molotti

CONFESSIONS OF A DOPE BOY
By Nicholas Lock

THA TAKEOVER
By Keith Chandler

BETRAYAL OF A G 2
By Ray Vinci

CRIME BOSS
By Playa Ray

Available Now

RESTRAINING ORDER 1 & 2
By **CA$H & Coffee**

LOVE KNOWS NO BOUNDARIES 1-3
By **Coffee**

RAISED AS A GOON I, II, III & IV
BRED BY THE SLUMS I, II, III
BLAST FOR ME I & II
ROTTEN TO THE CORE I II III
A BRONX TALE I, II, III
DUFFLE BAG CARTEL I II III IV V VI
HEARTLESS GOON I II III IV V
A SAVAGE DOPEBOY I II
DRUG LORDS I II III
CUTTHROAT MAFIA I II
KING OF THE TRENCHES
By **Ghost**

LAY IT DOWN I & II
LAST OF A DYING BREED I II
BLOOD STAINS OF A SHOTTA I & II III
By **Jamaica**

LOYAL TO THE GAME I II III
LIFE OF SIN I, II III
By **TJ & Jelissa**

IF LOVING HIM IS WRONG…I & II
LOVE ME EVEN WHEN IT HURTS I II III
By **Jelissa**

PUSH IT TO THE LIMIT
By **Bre' Hayes**

BLOODY COMMAS I & II
SKI MASK CARTEL I, II & III
KING OF NEW YORK I II, III IV V
RISE TO POWER I II III
COKE KINGS I II III IV V
BORN HEARTLESS I II III IV
KING OF THE TRAP I II
By **T.J. Edwards**

WHEN THE STREETS CLAP BACK I & II III
THE HEART OF A SAVAGE I II III IV
MONEY MAFIA I II
LOYAL TO THE SOIL I II III
By **Jibril Williams**

A DISTINGUISHED THUG STOLE MY HEART I II & III
LOVE SHOULDN'T HURT I II III IV
RENEGADE BOYS 1-4
PAID IN KARMA 1-3
SAVAGE STORMS 1-3
AN UNFORESEEN LOVE 1-3
BABY, I'M WINTERTIME COLD 1-3
A THUG'S STREET PRINCESS 1&2
By **Meesha**

A GANGSTER'S CODE 1-3
A GANGSTER'S SYN 1-3
THE SAVAGE LIFE 1-3
CHAINED TO THE STREETS 1-3
BLOOD ON THE MONEY 1-3
A GANGSTA'S PAIN 1-3
BEAUTIFUL LIES AND UGLY TRUTHS
CHURCH IN THESE STREETS
By **J-Blunt**

CUM FOR ME 1-8
An LDP Erotica Collaboration

BLOOD OF A BOSS 1-5
SHADOWS OF THE GAME
TRAP BASTARD
By **Askari**

THE STREETS BLEED MURDER 1-3
THE HEART OF A GANGSTA 1-3
By **Jerry Jackson**

WHEN A GOOD GIRL GOES BAD
By **Adrienne**

THE COST OF LOYALTY 1-3
By **Kweli**

BRIDE OF A HUSTLA 1-3
THE FETTI GIRLS 1-3
CORRUPTED BY A GANGSTA 1-4
BLINDED BY HIS LOVE
THE PRICE YOU PAY FOR LOVE 1-3
DOPE GIRL MAGIC 1-3
By **Destiny Skai**

A KINGPIN'S AMBITION
A KINGPIN'S AMBITION II
I MURDER FOR THE DOUGH
By **Ambitious**

TRUE SAVAGE 1-7
DOPE BOY MAGIC 1-3
MIDNIGHT CARTEL 1-3
CITY OF KINGZ 1&2
NIGHTMARE ON SILENT AVE
THE PLUG OF LIL MEXICO 1&2
CLASSIC CITY
By **Chris Green**

A GANGSTER'S REVENGE 1-4
THE BOSS MAN'S DAUGHTERS 1-5
A SAVAGE LOVE 1&2
BAE BELONGS TO ME 1&2
A HUSTLER'S DECEIT 1-3
WHAT BAD BITCHES DO 1-3
SOUL OF A MONSTER 1-3
KILL ZONE
A DOPE BOY'S QUEEN 1-3
TIL DEATH 1-3
IMMA DIE BOUT MINE 1-4
By **Aryanna**

A DOPEBOY'S PRAYER
By **Eddie "Wolf" Lee**

THE KING CARTEL 1-3
By **Frank Gresham**

THESE NIGGAS AIN'T LOYAL 1-3
By **Nikki Tee**

GANGSTA SHYT 1-3
By **CATO**

THE ULTIMATE BETRAYAL
By **Phoenix**

BOSS'N UP 1-3
By **Royal Nicole**

I LOVE YOU TO DEATH
By **Destiny J**

I RIDE FOR MY HITTA
I STILL RIDE FOR MY HITTA
By **Misty Holt**

LOVE & CHASIN' PAPER
By **Qay Crockett**

TO DIE IN VAIN
SINS OF A HUSTLA
By **ASAD**

BROOKLYN HUSTLAZ
By **Boogsy Morina**

BROOKLYN ON LOCK 1 & 2
By **Sonovia**

GANGSTA CITY
By **Teddy Duke**

A DRUG KING AND HIS DIAMOND 1-3
A DOPEMAN'S RICHES
HER MAN, MINE'S TOO 1&2
CASH MONEY HO'S
THE WIFEY I USED TO BE 1&2
PRETTY GIRLS DO NASTY THINGS
By **Nicole Goosby**

LIPSTICK KILLAH 1-3
CRIME OF PASSION 1-3
FRIEND OR FOE 1-3
By **Mimi**

TRAPHOUSE KING 1-3
KINGPIN KILLAZ 1-3
STREET KINGS 1&2
PAID IN BLOOD 1&2
CARTEL KILLAZ 1-3
DOPE GODS 1&2
By **Hood Rich**

THE STREETS ARE CALLING
By **Duquie Wilson**

STEADY MOBBN' 1-3
THE STREETS STAINED MY SOUL 1-3
By **Marcellus Allen**

WHO SHOT YA 1-3
SON OF A DOPE FIEND 1-4
HEAVEN GOT A GHETTO 1&2
SKI MASK MONEY 1&2
By **Renta**

GORILLAZ IN THE BAY 1-4
TEARS OF A GANGSTA 1/&2
3X KRAZY 1&2
STRAIGHT BEAST MODE 1&2
By **DE'KARI**

TRIGGADALE 1-3
MURDA WAS THE CASE 1-3
By **Elijah R. Freeman**

SLAUGHTER GANG 1-3
RUTHLESS HEART 1-3
By **Willie Slaughter**

GOD BLESS THE TRAPPERS 1-3
THESE SCANDALOUS STREETS 1-3
FEAR MY GANGSTA 1-5
THESE STREETS DON'T LOVE NOBODY 1-2
BURY ME A G 1-5
A GANGSTA'S EMPIRE 1-4
THE DOPEMAN'S BODYGAURD 1&2
THE REALEST KILLAZ 1-3
THE LAST OF THE OGS 1-3
By **Tranay Adams**

MARRIED TO A BOSS 1-3
By **Destiny Skai & Chris Green**

KINGZ OF THE GAME 1-7
CRIME BOSS 1-3
By **Playa Ray**

FUK SHYT
By **Blakk Diamond**

DON'T F#CK WITH MY HEART 1&2
By **Linnea**

ADDICTED TO THE DRAMA 1-3
IN THE ARM OF HIS BOSS
By **Jamila**

LOYALTY AIN'T PROMISED 1&2
By **Keith Williams**

YAYO 1-4
A SHOOTER'S AMBITION 1&2
BRED IN THE GAME
By **S. Allen**

TRAP GOD 1-3
RICH $AVAGE 1-3
MONEY IN THE GRAVE 1-3
CARTEL MONEY
By **Martell Troublesome Bolden**

FOREVER GANGSTA 1&2
GLOCKS ON SATIN SHEETS 1&2
By **Adrian Dulan**

TOE TAGZ 1-4
LEVELS TO THIS SHYT 1&2
IT'S JUST ME AND YOU
By **Ah'Million**

KINGPIN DREAMS 1-3
RAN OFF ON DA PLUG
By **Paper Boi Rari**

THE STREETS MADE ME 1-3
By **Larry D. Wright**

CONFESSIONS OF A GANGSTA 1-4
CONFESSIONS OF A JACKBOY 1-3
CONFESSIONS OF A HITMAN
By **Nicholas Lock**

I'M NOTHING WITHOUT HIS LOVE
SINS OF A THUG
TO THE THUG I LOVED BEFORE
A GANGSTA SAVED XMAS
IN A HUSTLER I TRUST
By **Monet Dragun**

QUIET MONEY 1-3
THUG LIFE 1-3
EXTENDED CLIP 1&2
A GANGSTA'S PARADISE
By **Trai'Quan**

CAUGHT UP IN THE LIFE 1-3
THE STREETS NEVER LET GO 1-3
By **Robert Baptiste**

NEW TO THE GAME 1-3
MONEY, MURDER & MEMORIES 1-3
By **Malik D. Rice**

CREAM 2-3
THE STREETS WILL TALK
By **Yolanda Moore**

THE STREETS WILL NEVER CLOSE 1-3
By **K'ajji**

LIFE OF A SAVAGE 1-4
A GANGSTA'S QUR'AN 1-4
MURDA SEASON 1-3
GANGLAND CARTEL 1-3
CHI'RAQ GANGSTAS 1-4
KILLERS ON ELM STREET 1-3
JACK BOYZ N DA BRONX 1-3
A DOPEBOY'S DREAM 1-3
JACK BOYS VS DOPE BOYS 1-3
COKE GIRLZ
COKE BOYS
SOSA GANG 1&2
BRONX SAVAGES
BODYMORE KINGPINS
BLOOD OF A GOON
By **Romell Tukes**

CONCRETE KILLA 1-3
VICIOUS LOYALTY 1-3
By **Kingpen**

THE ULTIMATE SACRIFICE 1-6
KHADIFI
IF YOU CROSS ME ONCE 1-3
ANGEL 1-4
IN THE BLINK OF AN EYE
By **Anthony Fields**

THE LIFE OF A HOOD STAR
By **Ca$h & Rashia Wilson**

NIGHTMARES OF A HUSTLA 1-3
BLOOD AND GAMES 1&2
By **King Dream**

GHOST MOB
By **Stilloan Robinson**

HARD AND RUTHLESS 1&2
MOB TOWN 251
THE BILLIONAIRE BENTLEYS 1-3
REAL G'S MOVE IN SILENCE
By **Von Diesel**

MOB TIES 1-7
SOUL OF A HUSTLER, HEART OF A KILLER 1-3
GORILLAZ IN THE TRENCHES
By **SayNoMore**

BODYMORE MURDERLAND 1-3
THE BIRTH OF A GANGSTER 1-4
By **Delmont Player**

FOR THE LOVE OF A BOSS 1&2
By **C. D. Blue**

KILLA KOUNTY 1-5
By **Khufu**

MOBBED UP 1-4
THE BRICK MAN 1-5
THE COCAINE PRINCESS 1-10
STEPPERS 1-3
SUPER GREMLIN 1-4
By **King Rio**

MONEY GAME 1&2
By **Smoove Dolla**

A GANGSTA'S KARMA 1-4
By **FLAME**

KING OF THE TRENCHES 1-3
By **GHOST & TRANAY ADAMS**

QUEEN OF THE ZOO 1&2
By **Black Migo**

GRIMEY WAYS 1-3
BETRAYAL OF A G
By **Ray Vinci**

XMAS WITH AN ATL SHOOTER
By **Ca$h & Destiny Skai**

KING KILLA 1&2
By **Vincent "Vitto" Holloway**

BETRAYAL OF A THUG 1&2
By **Fre$h**

THE MURDER QUEENS 1-5
By **Michael Gallon**

FOR THE LOVE OF BLOOD 1-4
By **Jamel Mitchell**

HOOD CONSIGLIERE 1&2
NO TIME FOR ERROR
By **Keese**

PROTÉGÉ OF A LEGEND 1&2
LOVE IN THE TRENCHES 1&2
By **Corey Robinson**

THE PLUG'S RUTHLESS DAUGHTER
By **Tony Daniels**

BORN IN THE GRAVE 1-3
CRIME PAYS
By **Self Made Tay**

MOAN IN MY MOUTH
By **XTASY**

TORN BETWEEN A GANGSTER AND A GENTLEMAN
By **J-BLUNT & Miss Kim**

LOYALTY IS EVERYTHING 1-3
CITY OF SMOKE 1&2
By **Molotti**

HERE TODAY GONE TOMORROW 1&2
By **Fly Rock**

WOMEN LIE MEN LIE 1-4
FIFTY SHADES OF SNOW 1-3
STACK BEFORE YOU SPLURGE
GIRLS FALL LIKE DOMINOES
NAÏVE TO THE STREETS
By **ROY MILLIGAN**

PILLOW PRINCESS
By **S. Hawkins**

THE BUTTERFLY MAFIA 1-3
SALUTE MY SAVAGERY 1&2
By **Fumiya Payne**

THE LANE 1&2
By Ken-Ken Spence

THE PUSSY TRAP 1-5
By **Nene Capri**

DIRTY DNA
By **Blaque**

SANCTIFIED AND HORNY
by **XTASY**

BOOKS BY LDP'S CEO, CA$H

TRUST IN NO MAN
TRUST IN NO MAN 2
TRUST IN NO MAN 3
BONDED BY BLOOD
SHORTY GOT A THUG
THUGS CRY
THUGS CRY 2
THUGS CRY 3
TRUST NO BITCH
TRUST NO BITCH 2
TRUST NO BITCH 3
TIL MY CASKET DROPS
RESTRAINING ORDER
RESTRAINING ORDER 2
IN LOVE WITH A CONVICT
LIFE OF A HOOD STAR
XMAS WITH AN ATL SHOOTER